W9-BND-529

HOW
ARE YOU
GOING
TO SAVE
YOURSELF

HOW ARE YOU GOING TO SAVE YOURSELF

JM HOLMES

Little, Brown and Company

New York Boston London

The characters and events in this book are fictitious. Any similarity to real persons, living or dead, is coincidental and not intended by the author.

Copyright © 2018 by JM Holmes

Hachette Book Group supports the right to free expression and the value of copyright. The purpose of copyright is to encourage writers and artists to produce the creative works that enrich our culture.

The scanning, uploading, and distribution of this book without permission is a theft of the author's intellectual property. If you would like permission to use material from the book (other than for review purposes), please contact permissions@hbgusa.com. Thank you for your support of the author's rights.

Little, Brown and Company
Hachette Book Group
1290 Avenue of the Americas, New York, NY 10104
littlebrown.com

First Edition: August 2018

Little, Brown and Company is a division of Hachette Book Group, Inc. The Little, Brown name and logo are trademarks of Hachette Book Group, Inc.

The following stories previously appeared, sometimes in different form, in these publications: "Everything Is Flammable" in the *Gettysburg Review;* "Kinfolk" in *H.O.W.;* "The Legend of Lonnie Lion" in the *Missouri Review;* "What's Wrong with You? What's Wrong with Me?" in the *Paris Review;* and "Cookouts" in *The White Review.*

Lyrics on the first and last pages of "Toll for the Passengers" are from "Sing About Me, I'm Dying of Thirst" by Kendrick Lamar Duckworth, Gabriel Stevenson, Derrick Hutchins, Quincy Jones, Alan Bergman, and Marilyn Bergman; the lines of poetry about gunfire in "Outside Tacoma" are from "Someday I'll Love Ocean Vuong" by Ocean Vuong, from *Night Sky with Exit Wounds;* and the Nina Simone lyrics in "Kinfolk" are from "Feeling Good" by Anthony Newley and Leslie Bricusse.

The publisher is not responsible for websites (or their content) that are not owned by the publisher.

The Hachette Speakers Bureau provides a wide range of authors for speaking events. To find out more, go to hachettespeakersbureau.com or call (866) 376-6591.

ISBN 978-0-316-51488-0
LCCN 2018931946

10 9 8 7 6 5 4 3 2 1

LSC-C

Printed in the United States of America

For the dearly beloved ghosts

Contents

What's Wrong with You? What's Wrong with Me?   3

The Legend of Lonnie Lion   19

Be Good to Me   47

Toll for the Passengers   81

Kinfolk   101

Outside Tacoma   125

Everything Is Flammable   151

Dress Code   183

Cookouts   217

HOW ARE YOU GOING TO SAVE YOURSELF

WHAT'S WRONG WITH YOU? WHAT'S WRONG WITH ME?

How many white women you been with?"

The room was filled with good smoke and we drifted off behind it.

"What's your number?" Dub looked at Rye real serious like he was asking about his mom's health.

I leaned forward from the couch and took the burning nub of joint from his outstretched hand. We called him Dub because his name was Lazarus Livingston—double L. His parents named him to be a football star. He could play once upon a time, but not like Rye.

Rolls, who was too high, chimed in: "Stop it, bruh, that shit's not important."

"Yeah, it is. I'm finna touch every continent," Dub said.

"White's not a continent," Rolls said.

"You know what I mean."

"I know you never won a geography bee," Rolls said.

The room was streaked with haze like we dropped cream in a coffee, but Rolls never cracked any windows. He smoked like a pro even still, burned blunts and let the smoke box out the room. He had the leather furniture from his dad's old office at the camera shop and we sank into it. His new place was nice, on the north end of Blackstone but before you hit the old-money houses on the east side of Providence. These days, he got lit every morning before work, after his bowl of Smacks. His latest gig was shooting an ad for the ambulance chaser Anthony Izzo. I was about to ask him if he still painted.

"Why won't you answer the question?" Dub continued. "Gio would answer." He looked at me. "Wouldn't you, G?"

"Don't play this game," I said.

"How many?"

"Man, G don't count," Rye said. "He's mixed—that's a performance-enhancing drug." He tagged me light on the chest.

"He speaks!" Dub said.

"Shut the fuck up," Rye said.

"Chill with that," Rolls said. "My place is a sanctuary."

"Stop with the Buddhist bullshit," Dub said.

I put the joint out. Rye started rolling another.

Rolls stood but put his hand on the armrest to steady himself. "It's Brahman," he said.

"Brah—shut-the-fuck-up," Rye said.

Rolls smacked his lips and looked at Rye. "You two belong together," he said. "I'm getting a drink."

"Get me one," I said.

Rolls wiped his eyes and left to the kitchen.

"Really, though, why you being shy?" Dub nudged Rye. Their huge frames looked goofy on the couch together, boulders sinking into the leather, jostling each other like idiots.

"Nigga, stop, I'm rolling. You'll ruin the J."

"My Gawd! You've never fucked a white chick."

"Don't be stupid."

"You haven't."

Rye began licking the edges and shaking the cone down.

"Don't pack it too tight," I said.

"Madie teach you that?" Rye said.

Rye knew I didn't roll well, but my girl rolled Js better than him and Rolls. She kept the J loose enough to pull well but tight enough not to burn sloppy or canoe. I loved watching her manicured fingers at work. The first time I brought her back to the city and showed her the spots, she rolled our weed and talked above us, underneath us, and around us. My boys cracked jokes and looked out for her. They treated her like a long-lost, porcelain-colored cousin. She said our outdoor weed was garbage. We called it middies. She called it schwag. Both equated to "trash." Rye said that Madie was the first woman he ever bought a drink for, but I'd seen his lying ass spend money on chicks in high school.

Madie liked the area so much that she decided to live there when she got a finance job offer in Foxborough a few years later. The commute was about twenty minutes, but she said the money saved on rent was worth it. I didn't buy it. She wanted to prove she could hang.

"That's one hell of a white girl," Rye said.

"Don't change the subject. We're talking about you," I said.

"How is the old lady?" Dub said.

"Nah, this about him," I said.

Dub pulled on his nose the way he did when he was thinking of some heinous shit. "I just wanna know how the treads are," he said.

"Yeah, how's it hittin'?" Rye said.

I leveled my eyes at him. "Don't talk about my girl like that."

"Stop being soft," Dub said.

"He's Team Light-Skinned," Rye said. "Let him be."

"You're a fucking macadamia nut," I said.

They both were silent a second, then started laughing.

"Y'all are stupid," I said.

"Sing me a love song, Urkel," Dub said.

Rye looked away. Rolls returned and handed me my drink. It tasted like straight Coke and I told him.

"Strength is life, weakness is death," he said.

"Man, I don't even know why we come here," Rye said.

"'Cause you're scared of your landlord." Rolls took the joint from him.

"Gandhi's got jokes," Rye said.

Rye's landlord was a fat Irishman with an absurdly thick neck. He didn't mind Rye moving in because he remembered watching him take the team to a state football title back in the day. Now Rye kept his music low and entered the house without switching on the stair light when he came home real late. We could never smoke at his spots, even growing up. At his mother's house, we couldn't smoke because she'd wake up and press us for some. Rye would pretend it didn't bother him, but she'd start wringing her hands and glancing around because she wanted more than trees, and I would stick my head in the fridge and pretend there was something there to look at.

"My boy's not scared of that fat-ass mick," Dub said. "But he's clearly scared of white pussy."

"Let it rest," I said.

"Fear is at the center of all hate," Rolls said.

"You're smoked out," Dub said.

Rolls passed me the joint and got up to throw on a track. In middle school, Rye and I used to bump Dipset, wasting our freshman highs on rap with one dimension—sped-up drums, pitch-altered samples chopped up and arranged to bang like gunshots. We would smoke weed in my aunt Mary's basement because she worked a lot and was hardly home. We sprayed air freshener and enjoyed the cool mist on our skin as we walked through and back in a daze. She never came down even when she was home, but we sprayed it anyway.

One day, Rye left upstairs to go to the bathroom and didn't come back. I waited awhile, letting the minutes bend around me and grow fat as I climbed into the high. I thought I heard a door shut. I sprayed more, thinking it was my aunt, home early for some reason. I tripped up the stairs, boots heavier than usual. No one was in the kitchen–living room. There were some orange peels. Rye always ate my food. He said football players needed the calories. I wondered if he'd gone to 7-Eleven for more snacks, but his coat was still on the counter. I went by the bathroom—door open, fan still on. Computer room—empty, but the computer was loading. I sat down to see what recruiting videos he was watching, but after a minute, he hadn't returned. I went into the hall. My aunt's door was open. I went to bust in and scare the shit out of him but came up quiet inside my high. In the room, he moved around slow, stopping by her dresser and studying the pictures. He picked up one of her standing next to her flavor of the year, Luca, on a beach in Rio. She looked tan in her purple bikini. Rye stared for a while. Then he reached his hand to open the top drawer of the dresser.

"What the fuck!" I said.

Rye was so shook he banged his knee on the shelf. "Shit!" he said. "Why you sneaking up on me?"

"The fuck you doing?"

"I got lost," he said.

"You're not that high."

He sat on the bed, rubbing his knee.

I gestured at the drawer. "That shit is weird," I said.

He stood and set the photograph upright again. Paused. "She's sexy, man."

I slapped him on the back of the head. He made like he was going to tag me in the chest. I flinched. I made like I was going to tag him back. He flinched too.

"She got those green eyes," he said.

"Fuck's wrong with you?"

He paused like the question was philosophical. "I been conditioned," he said.

I cut my eyes at him. "Don't—"

"My conditioning has been conditioned." He smirked.

"Ya funny," I said. I didn't feel like picking up what he was putting down and looked at my aunt's pictures, then out the window instead.

Rolls cranked up the Impressions—*So people get ready, for the train to Jordan*. I loved that song, but I was surprised Rye and Dub let it ride. Years ago, Dub would've cut it off and tried to convince us to hit the clubs on Westminster, but we'd have wound up at a house party with jungle juice and dancehall playing instead. Now, we got higher and thought ahead to Thanksgiving, about chopping it up with whatever family we had left.

Rolls had his attempts at abstract art hung on the walls. Maybe it was the smoke, or the way the red, green, and white paint seemed to pop over the black roofing material, but the work was actually beautiful, balanced.

"He won't tell us 'cause he ain't been with any," Dub said.

"How many have *you* been with?" Rye said.

"Too many to count." Dub smiled.

"Stop lyin'."

"I like to take 'em in the shower." Dub grinned. "Let 'em bathe me," he said.

"You watch too much porn," I said.

"I even had this one, Cici, after she finished washing me, she hit me with the Eddie Murphy line."

"Bullshit," Rye said.

"Real talk. She said, 'The royal penis is clean, Your Highness.'"

"You're lyin'," Rye said.

"Why would I lie?"

"You add to the mischief of the world," Rolls said.

I liked to wash Madie's hair when we were in the shower together. The way it trapped water and became heavy satin in my hands. It went all the way down to her lower back. She thought mine was waterproof. Her shampoo smelled of sweet citrus and vanilla. She let her hair air-dry in the kitchen while she made steel-cut oats with flax for breakfast. I drenched the hippie shit in syrup and told her how good it was.

"Yeah, aight," Rye said.

"I just treat 'em how they wanna be treated. Choke the daddy issues out of 'em. If they want me to play Dominican, I let 'em call me Papi. Anything but gentle. Long as you know that, you're straight."

"Lyin' ass—" Rye started.

"Don't be mad at me," Dub said. "You should really do better for yourself. You played ball."

"I've fucked white women," Rye said.

"Then just tell us how many."

"I'm out if you don't stop," I said.

Rye took a deep pull from his drink. It wasn't his pace.

"You ain't gotta be mad. We ain't talkin' about Madie," Dub said.

When Dub and I used to slap-box in high school, Rye would always break it up before we close-fisted each other. Dub said I was too pretty to throw hands anyway. I told him his bulky ass was too slow to fade me. He'd say, *Light-skins bruise like fruit.*

"You think she been keeping herself pure for you?" Dub said.

"Easy, Dub," Rolls said.

"You think some big motherfucker ain't coming around to hit it right while you're not here."

I stood up. Dub leaned forward.

"And you think Simone faithful to your lame ass?" I said.

He brushed some ash off his long leg. "Keep my girl's name out your mouth."

"Dub, fall back," Rolls said.

I kept my eyes locked on Dub. "Who's whipped now?" I said.

The music changed tracks and went on. Old Cole.

"Nigga, you sweet—"

I slapped the joint out of his mouth before he could finish. He was halfway up when Rye grabbed him in a bear hug, there on the couch. Dub threw his elbows a few times trying to break free.

"Calm down," Rye said. "Calm down."

"Nah, this nigga thinks his girl isn't community property. It's a revolving door when you ain't around, Captain Save-a-Ho. You the only nigga that kiss that bitch on the mouth."

I tried to get close enough to swing, but Rolls had gotten up and was standing in the way.

"Calm the fuck down," Rye said. "Leave," he said to me.

"Fuck that—"

"I *know* niggas that piped!" Dub said.

I lunged and swung at his face, but at the last moment Rolls tried to step in front and tripped on the table. My knuckles landed on the side of his jaw. I felt the connection like when the baseball hits the sweet spot of the bat—it caves with a softness. Rolls fell against Rye, then into the couch. Blood already outlined his teeth. Rye and Dub still struggled. I didn't know whether to apologize or keep swinging. I felt like I was in a pool of water and my limbs were weak and slow. Then Rolls kicked me in the shin with his heel.

"Go!" he said. "Get the fuck out."

IT WAS COLD out and leaves scratched down the block. Rye said that Rolls was fine. We were faded. The night was dark. We headed toward East Ave. Back toward Rye's. It wasn't rough like Prospect Heights, where he came up, but he still wanted a nicer place where he and his girl, Marissa, could live together. Rye stumbled a little bit, leaving the glow of the orange streetlight and falling into shadow for a moment.

"I haven't had an empanada in a while," I said.

"Yeah," he said, "you've been gone a minute." His voice sounded far off. A car wheeled by with windows rattling.

"So were you."

Rye stopped, burped, and let it out into the night like dragon fire. He took a quick right into the backstreets. I tripped a little trying to follow him.

"Forget the shortcuts?" he said.

Stefano's yellow awning came up on the right, a high man's

beacon to buñuelos and ramen hot enough to peel the weed film off our tongues—that was high school. The inside smelled the same as always—grease and incense. The baked goods in the case had gone cold, but if you told them you were going to eat it then, they fired it up hot for you. I got two chicken empanadas and a potato one for Rye. He thought they filled you up more. The man behind the counter was too tall for his job. He threw the goods in the toaster and turned the knob, then went back to his magazine.

"Drew still work here?" I asked.

He looked up. "Who?"

We stared at each other for a moment. "Forget it," I said, but he was back in the pages.

I thought about getting a strawberry soda. My tongue felt thick. I eyed the Game wraps and thought about when we'd cut class to smoke in Slater Park—hotbox the car, then get the five-dollar special at East Buffet while the Chinese workers eyed us like we were going to dine-and-dash on them.

"Put the potato one in a separate bag," I said.

Outside, Rye looked at the bag a long time before saying he didn't want it.

"C'mon, we're lit. You're starving," I said.

"I'm not hungry."

"I don't even fuck with the potato ones," I said.

"I'm not fuckin' hungry."

"Stop acting shady," I said.

"Shady?" He laughed. "What are we, in middle school?"

"Strange, weird, suspect, indignant. What the fuck you want me to say?"

"Say my name, say my name," he belted into the night.

I was about to clown him for singing but started eating instead. The chicken ones were too good and I was too hungry to wait for his bullshit to cease. They were hot all the way through. I missed cutting class to come grab a bagful with Rye, talking about which coaches were after him. The day he got a letter from Morehead State, his mom broke down and started thanking God, even though she wasn't religious like that. He was going to school for free. I bought bottles and we found a nice spot on the river, mixed Hpnotiq with Henney, threw it all on ice and drank until we couldn't feel summer's absence.

"You know he woulda laid you out, right?" he said.

"What?"

"Dub. He woulda beat your ass."

I put the crust of my empanada back in the bag and stared at him. "Fuck him, I—"

"Nah." Rye cut me off. "He woulda fucked you up."

"You got something you want to say?"

"Why you mad?" he said.

"Why'd you stop him, then?"

He looked off. "'Cause I didn't know you were gonna swing on Rolls."

I flexed my fist and thought about Rolls, bloody-mouthed on the floor. I wished my car wasn't parked at Rye's. Madie would be waiting. She hated when I came home lit, but she liked getting lit with me. I visited her place so many weekends that we were trying to figure out how to move in together. Our time was like repeated honeymoons, languid and blissful—ordering food, frantic sex before, taking our time with the thing after, falling asleep in ways that only we knew, having worked them out together night after night until we fitted like matryoshkas.

He quit smiling and watched the stoplight at the top of the hill. The city was built on hills, with roads that curved and ended abruptly and led deeper and deeper into a labyrinth split by a snaking river that changed color with the season 'cause of the dye left over from the textiles back in the day.

"I did sleep with one white girl," Rye said.

I crumpled my bag from the market and tossed it, wiped my mouth with the back of my hand. "Why didn't you just say?"

He sped up a little and I lengthened my stride to follow.

"None of that shit would've happened," I said.

"Fuck you, you should've fought him forever ago."

"He roasts niggas, that's just what he does," I said.

He eased up on the pace. "I'm just playin'. I didn't sleep with no white bitch."

"What the fuck is wrong with you?" I said. "What happened?"

"Nothing."

"Bro, remember when I caught you looking through my aunt's panties?"

He shot me a look, then smiled. "What had happened was—"

"Man, shut up." The wind picked up to bring winter faster. "Whatever it is can't be that bad."

"Aight," he said. He glanced over at me. "Well, in the middle of it…" he started.

We were at the stoplight. There were no cars. He bounced into the street. I followed.

"When I was hittin'."

"Yeah?" I tried to catch up.

"She called me a nigger."

I fell behind a step, then two.

"That's fucked up." It was all I could say.

I thought about if Madie pulled some shit like that. I thought about the type of white women who went out in search of that, the ones who kept the word in the backs of their throats—an ugly appetite. Madie wasn't like that—guilt maybe, that was this country, but nothing dank and malignant. I thought back to when we'd looked at each other in the mirror together, floor-length at her parents' in Manhattan, her smiling with a hand around my dick. I tried for a minute to see what she saw. I told myself I wasn't on an auction block in front of her.

"Rye," I said.

He woke up.

"And?"

I reached the left onto his street before he did. Still he was silent, trying to lock something inside, back where it belonged. He grew fidgety in the shadow of the streetlight.

"Yo," I said.

He turned. "I liked it," he said.

"Liked what?"

"When she said it." He paused. "I fuckin' liked it."

"How?"

"It made me harder."

We neared his steps.

"Like—hardened your resolve to find a strong black woman?" I raised my fist.

He left the joke in space.

I stopped as we reached his stairs.

"You're not staying?" he said.

"Nah, man."

He toed a spot where the stair was chipped and splintered.

"Over that shit?"

I handed him the bag with his empanada. "I just want to see Madie," I said.

He put his hand on the rail before he turned to go up and paused. "I loved it," he said. "It made me an animal."

"Yeah."

"No, you don't understand, man. I grabbed her hair and turned her face away. I don't know." He took a breath. "I wouldn't even let her look at me. She said it again—*Fuck me like a nigger*." He stared at the ground for a while. "I wanted her so bad," he said. "She tried to turn her face toward me and I just buried it deeper. I thought I was going to break her. It's like I couldn't stop. I shoved my fingers down her throat with my other hand and she closed her eyes. I wouldn't even let her do that. I raised her eyelid so she had to keep an eye open. I bit her jaw until I saw teeth marks." He brushed his hand over his waves like he'd always done. "I lost my mind."

He went up the first step. The automatic porch light came on. I imagined him walking up the stairs to the second floor in the pitch-black. Going home to no one, eating his food alone.

"Then it worked," I said.

"What?"

I took a few steps back. "She got what she wanted."

He held the paper bag tighter, glared like he was going to start something, then his eyes softened. "Say hi to Madie for me."

I let the words hang in the night. As I turned the corner toward my car, I heard the apartment door close.

THE LEGEND OF LONNIE LION

Two pieces of my pops' advice stuck with me—*Don't marry a white girl*, and *Never pick the skin off chicken—it's the best part.* I don't pick the skin off of chicken 'cause he was right about that. And even though it was just my pops playing around, I can't see the first piece of advice sitting well with my mom, Nicoletta.

LONNIE CAMPBELL COULD run so fast. Lonnie could hit so hard.

MY POPS WAS big enough to block doorways, and Mom was small enough to almost fit her whole body into one of his pant legs. It's hard for me to imagine them together. They met back at the University of Washington. She was his tutor, but really she wrote essays for players on the Huskies football team to pay her tuition. Pops grew up an army brat and spent some time on Fort McChord when Big Daddy, his father, was stationed there. It made sense for him to stay in Washington. How my mom, an East Coast girlie, ended up in Washington, I still don't know. She doesn't speak much on it but always yells "U Dub!" every time she sees someone rocking the gear, and I shake my head.

He left the university a year early to turn pro. Mom was a year ahead so it worked out. He was a D-end, first for the Tampa Bay Bucs and then for the San Francisco 49ers. My mom took the football bread that was coming in and became a self-taught architect and real-estate developer. She made some investments, made money—at least, that's how she tells it. But she had Italian hustle like that so I buy it. I don't know many stories from the bliss times. I know that she played tennis well, and after I was born, my pops got a few sets in with her every day so she could lose that baby weight and get back in shape. Afterward, they'd bike through the burnt-out California hills, those rose-gold, cracked slopes that jutted up between the houses and kept all the lives private. My pops is fat as shit now.

I was around six when they split—before I can really remember. His body was too shot to keep playing football, and he left to try and make some moves in LA. Mom got us a studio in Korea-town to stay close. For reasons I didn't understand, the money was all gone. My mom and I slept in the same bed together with a baseball bat next to the nightstand. No one ever broke in and Pops never came back.

After LA had squeezed him for the last of his football dollars, Pops moved back up to Washington and had a kid, my little sister Whitney, with his high-school sweetheart. I was around nine then and our communication went radio silent for a while. My mom and I fled east to Rhode Island to be with her mascarpone-colored family. But some years later, when I was old enough to fly alone, she would still send me to visit my pops, would buy the plane tickets and drive me to the airport. She never tripped over the lack of child support and even smiled each time she walked me to the terminal. The smiles were always nervous—*Come back you, the you I've been building for years. Come back the way I've made you.* Pops would send me back with my suitcase filled with FUBU and Coogi off the discount racks, clothes my mom *accidentally* ruined in the wash.

THE SUMMER I was thirteen I clocked the Sea-Tac Airport for the first time. Pops was waiting at the gate in beat-up loafers and sweats. That's the way he rocked, comfortable, the years of football stardom long gone. Back in his playing days, he used to wear suits to games, but I guess sometime after the lights dimmed and the yelling stopped and the bones in his battered knees ground like pestles into mortars, he wanted something more forgiving.

His massive frame drew stares as he scooped me up. I tried to keep my feet planted, play it cool, but it's hard to resist a forklift. In a too-loud voice he said, "Let me smell ya, make sure you're my cub." Then he dug his uneven beard into my neck and made snorting noises. I laughed despite myself. He let me down, said I was the right one, and we left those people at the gate.

After he threw my suitcase in the trunk of his old DeVille, he squeezed himself into the driver's seat and started the car. I brushed some cracker crumbs off the leather and put my bag next to Whit's car seat in the back. Pops was a shitty driver. His legs were too long and got tangled beneath the wheel. (He got his license revoked later, but not for that.) After he turned the radio on, he accelerated into horns and oncoming traffic.

"So what kind of music you into now?" he asked.

"Rap."

"C'mon, G-Money, you gotta tell me more than that. Who you listen to?"

"I dunno."

"What you mean, *you dunno?*" he mumbled, trying to clown me.

The state grew greener as we headed south on I-5 toward Olympia.

"I like Dipset," I said.

"You ain't listen to my man Ricky Ross?"

"He's okay."

Pops looked over at me. The car swerved a little. "You know if I was a rapper, I'd be like Rick Ross."

I nodded.

"You know why?"

"'Cause you're both fat?" I said.

"You think I'm fat? Your cousins call me Uncle Love Biscuits. I only stay big for them."

"Okay," I said.

"If they didn't like it, I'd be lean and fast as my playing days. They used to call me Lonnie 'Lion' Campbell."

"Dad, you look more like a rhino." I blew out my cheeks like a puffer fish.

He stared over at me real serious. "You don't believe me?"

The highway got wider once we were south of Tacoma, and the people drove slower. I liked when my pops talked about his NFL days. He got animated and used my name for dramatic effect—Gio, G, G-Money, or, when he told his tallest tales, Giovanni.

"Are you dunking yet?"

"I'm thirteen."

"I was dunking by thirteen," he said.

"Sure."

"I could still dunk now, G, that's God-given. Just 'cause I got some fat on these muscles don't mean the muscles ain't there."

I glanced over at my pops, the way his tan sweats rode up,

stuffed into the driver's seat of the DeVille, he looked like a goofy-ass chocolate sundae drenched in caramel. I broke out laughing. My pops was funny when he lied. Maybe that's why he got away with it his whole life.

MY STEPMOM, DEE, Pops' second woman, or the second I'd met, smoked cigarettes. They were brown and longer than straws and she'd stand outside forever in the summer breeze burning them down to the last. We got along all right as I grew a little older. Pops and I were still drifting back toward each other and I wasn't going to let anyone mess it up. So on Sundays, to bond, I would even ride with Dee an hour to the Indian reservation, where she could buy her cartons tax-free. But back in the duplex, whenever she left them on the counter, I'd hide them in the big vase near the front door. There must have been thirty packs in there she never found. She used to bitch and blame my pops. He never yelled at me, though. He didn't want her to smoke anyway and I just wanted to be a punk.

TWO YEARS LATER, the summer I was fifteen, I saw Dee walk out of the bathroom in just a towel. I'd been watching preseason football on the TV in their bedroom 'cause that's where the cable box was. She walked like she deserved everything and let her towel fall in front of the mirror. She was the right kind of full. The girls at my school were starting to grow up, but her figure still looked alien—her hair in two long braids that almost reached her ass, which curved and sat in place thicker than a basketball.

"Jay Stephens used to come by the house when I was in high school," she said, nodding toward the TV, her voice hissing like rain on a campfire.

I didn't even turn back to see who she was talking about. Before I had a chance to take it all in, my little sister came into the room and jumped on the bed with me.

"Put *Lilo* on," she said.

I changed the channel to Disney. The smell of beeswax came off her hair.

"You just get braided?"

She smiled and whipped her braids around, letting the beaded ends bounce off each other. "Audrey says I'm gonna be a heart taker."

"Heart*breaker*."

But she wasn't listening to me. The Jonas Brothers were on the TV. She loved kid pop stars like her mom loved athletes, and I prayed she didn't grow up to be a groupie.

Then my pops walked in, big and calm. He smacked Dee's ass and it rippled like a pot of hot water before it boils.

She pushed him away. "Not in front of the kids!" She wrapped herself in the towel again.

"What?" My pops had a hoarse laugh that came from deep inside him. He grabbed her around the waist and she pushed him away again. Then he caught me watching. "C'mon, G-Money, don't act like you ain't never seen one before." He laughed again.

I looked back at the TV. "I seen plenty," I said.

"Boy, you ain't seen none," Dee said. Then she dropped her own laugh on me and I shrank inside.

"Whitney, show your brother the new paint job in your room," my pops said.

"I wanna go to the store," I said.

"And?" he said.

"Let me use the car."

"Let me see your license," he said.

"Mom has me drive." That wasn't a lie. She'd let me get my permit early, but every time in the car with me, she still sweat the whole ride like the next hog in line.

"You better start walking," Dee said.

They were already fooling around by the time I got up and took my sister out of the room with me.

Whitney didn't play sports. At age five, she was all diva already. The walls of her room were painted light pink and periwinkle. My pops had painted the walls twice but painted them again when she didn't like the shade of pink. She spent the next hour showing me toys, and I fell asleep on her bed surrounded by stuffed animals.

My mom and I moved around Rhode Island a lot while she got certified and chased teaching jobs. She stopped developing real estate, said it was 'cause she wanted to be home more, but I think there was no more football money. In small-town middle schools, I fell in love with some freckled girls in light-up sneakers and wasted my lunch money on giant Hershey's Kisses for them, trying to steal a kiss—Dee would've called me a trick. Even when the kiddie-love dates never seemed to work out, my age kept me ignorant to hate-eyed parents. Mom said nothing and kept us moving, looking for a better place.

When I got to high school, I fell hard for one Saba Thomas, a light-skinned Cape Verdean girl who had my nose wide open. My mom tried to keep me safe from the blaze. She didn't like when I hung out in neighborhoods like Saba's—everything in Spanish or Portuguese, police curfews, kids all ages mobbing on corners. She was always confusing safety for happiness. She still is. But she tried to like the girls once I brought them home.

The only girls I brought home were ones my pops would've said had "the potion." He would try to move his hips like a merengue dancer and tap his ass while he said it. "Campbells can't fight the good potion," he said. I still remember that. I still think about Saba.

She liked my voice. You talk so sexy, she said.

We had *How High* blaring from the TV to drown out the sounds of us flirting and drinking. Still, I listened for her mom moving in the next room.

Yeah?

Yeah, say something.

What do you want me to say? I felt like I was whispering.

Anything. Surprise me.

What do you mean, anything?

Jesus, just shut up, she said.

I never had game. I went to kiss her and she lay back on the couch, playing like she was trying to avoid me. Back then, everything happened on couches. Bedrooms were never vacant. She shared a room with her little sister, and her mom and step-pops had the other one, even though he was never home. Her skin was almond, and the shape of her gets fuller the longer it brews in my memory. I remember her hips hatching out of her jeans and the soft lines of her slender shoulders.

Won't your mom wake up? I said.

My mom's a drunk.

Drinks don't put me to sleep.

Then you don't drink enough, she said, and kissed me. Are you drunk now? she asked.

Should I be?

She puckered her lips at me. Her skin stretched tight at her temples like a drum. I looked down at the empty pint of rum we'd gotten from the A+.

I'm tipsy, I said.

She bit me.

Fuck! I said.

No, you're not, she said and got up off the couch. She took off her shirt in that cross-armed way, exposing her smooth café con leche skin. In only her panties, she walked around the wall to the kitchen. I followed but trying to slide in slow, like my pops. The kitchen was a narrow strip separated from the TV room by a small round table. I was tall enough to see on top of the fridge, where her mom hid the box of Fruity Pebbles from her younger sister. Saba went for the wine rack on the counter and pulled a bottle with a dusty French label.

Damn, that's old, I said.

It's my grandmother's.

She grabbed a bottle opener and uncorked it.

Really? I asked.

Stop being a pussy, she said. My mom won't notice.

She drank from the bottle in deep pulls, spilling enough that it ran all the way from the corners of her lips down her neck and chest to her stomach, staining the white edge of her underwear. The green stripes, dark and fine, didn't show it as much. I tried to take the bottle, but she held on to it and danced around— curves and hips and black hair.

Here. She handed me the bottle and kissed me with purple lips.

I sipped it.

Drink it, she said.

I'm good, I said.

I didn't know you were such a bitch.

I tipped the bottle back again. The wine was sweet and warm.

More, she said.

I drank till there were only sips left to swirl at the bottom and set the bottle down. She grabbed my cold hands, lifted them up, and twirled underneath my arms. She moved in circles with her waist—her eyes took everything into their black. We danced for a while in silence. I started to feel warm in the fingers and bent down and lifted her up.

Good, she said, and she kissed on my neck.

I let her down and she opened the door on their fourth-story porch. She flung the empty bottle over the railing and the glass shattered across the parking lot with a pop.

Ay, maricón, someone yelled, looking up at us.

Yo, no speaki español. She smiled and grabbed below my belt. I smacked her ass. She was too thin to ripple.

AFTER PROMOTING BOXING, Pops tried to start a clothing line, then a recording label. It all went belly-up, and the football money vanished. He started cleaning office buildings at night with my uncle Bull, his brother-in-law. He claimed my mom resented him for not taking the NFL insurance money when he had the chance, but she never said as much to me, and, to her credit, even when we were living off my grandmother while my mom went back to school, she never came after my pops for the piece of nothing he had.

The days after his night shifts, he'd sleep till dinner, so I wound up spending more of the summer with my sister and Dee.

I grew to like Dee. She acted younger than she should have, but my pops did too, so it all failed just right.

During the summer after my sophomore year, she started chopping it up with me about weed and tattoos and I thought that was cool. One day, she finally gassed me into wanting one, then said she'd take me.

The whole way there Whitney talked about all the tats she was going to get when she was old enough. She was only seven. Dee said nothing, blew smoke from her long cigarette out the window, and laughed hollow like she was far away.

The spot we pulled up to wasn't a shop. It was a house. Dee had called twice on the way but no one had picked up.

"Maybe he's busy," I said.

"We'll wait."

The duplex had a bunch of cars out front.

"We could just go to a real place," I said.

"Stop acting shook."

We walked up to the front door and rang the bell. A dude with good tattoos on his neck and arms and the worst tattoos I'd ever seen on his legs answered.

"Yeah?"

"Mando here?"

"Who's asking?"

"Tell him it's Deandra."

"Aight, hold on." He disappeared into music and barking.

A short, dark Asian came to the door next. "Damn, Dee, look at you, still fine as hell."

Dee laughed and they hugged. "How are things?" she said.

"Not bad. Been a little tough since I lost the shop but they still spread the good word."

"I can see that." Dee glanced back at all the cars on the lawn. "You look real busy."

"Nah, half these cars are just sack chasers here to buy movies from Quintin." He stared out into the yard at his grass burnt brown from the summer heat. Then looked at the sky like he was waiting for rain and the cool northwest breeze that blew when the sun started to go down.

"How long's the wait? My kid wants some work done."

"Little Whitney?" He smiled.

"Boy, stop. Lonnie's kid."

Mando looked me over like I was an ink-blot test. "Okay. I gotta finish up homeboy that's in the chair now and then I can hook him up." He moved aside and we all walked in. The walls inside were hung with modern art, and 808 drum kicks pulsed from everything. Muted music videos were playing on a box flat-screen TV, and the two leather couches were packed with people. Mando got jittery for a second. "Ay, turn that shit down," he said. "We got kids in here now. Put that dutch out too."

"I just sparked it."

"Fuck, nigga, then take it outside."

I wanted to tell them they could smoke inside, I wanted to evaporate into the tree clouds with them. To the left of the couches, away from the TV, a man lay facedown on a table with towels taped to it. The towels had been white once but were now smudged across with black ink. Mando's fingers were eternally black. He reached to pick up the needle and shuddered, then went to the bathroom for a long time.

I sat and looked at the binders of his work. Unlike most artists', Mando's had no photos. The binder was filled with paintings and sketches and notes on napkins.

The man with the bad and good tattoos came and sat next to me on the couch. "He's nice, right?" He pointed to the binder.

"Yeah, dude is real nice," I said.

"I don't think you appreciate—Mando's a fuckin' maestro, kid."

I fixed my eyes on his bad tattoos, but the way he kept tapping his feet moved their uneven lines and made me sick.

"What's with those?" I said, pointing to the half-sketched faces above his knee.

"Oh." He laughed. "He's teaching me. These are my practice runs."

"You couldn't get a dummy or some shit?"

"Mando believes in learning on the job. That's how you get nice. Not with fuckin' dummies."

I wanted to ask him if he knew that his shitty tattoos were permanent, but his eyes bounced around like something was pressing them out from the inside. He made me nervous.

Mando came out of the bathroom and closed the door behind him. Whitney sat on a plastic folding chair playing on her chunky red Game Boy, and Dee had squeezed herself between some dudes on the other couch. She was rocking the Cleopatra weave those days and the men were licking their lips and leaning too close.

Soon enough, Mando was done and the man got up from the raised table. He walked over to the mirror to inspect the deep black lines of a crucifix that seemed big enough to weigh him down. The Jesus was tragic and Latin-looking. The cross was beautiful and seemed to raise off his back like it was somehow staring down from above even if you were looking straight at it. The whole picture came off graceful, even with the deep, painful lines of Christ's wounded body.

Mando came up to me and nodded toward the table.

I walked over and Dee got up from her fans and followed.

"What do you want?" Mando said.

"People are trapped in history and history is trapped in them."

He cut his eyes at Dee. "You ain't tell me all he wanted was a quote."

"In script," I said.

Dee stared at me. "I didn't know," she said.

"That shit's a waste of my time."

"Why don't you get some art?" Dee said.

"'Cause I want a quote." I couldn't think of anything else I wanted.

He sighed. "What's it again?"

"People are trapped in history and history is trapped in them."

He glanced at Dee. "Where the fuck you find this kid?"

"I don't know. He's Lonnie's kid. He's half white."

They laughed.

"You're open." Mando shook his head. "Who said that?" he asked.

"James Baldwin."

"*Who?*"

I was silent for a while, listening to them roast me.

Then Mando got real irritable again. "I ain't dealin' with this shit," he said.

"Relax," Dee said.

"It's a waste of my day. I, I, I try and do you a favor—" He stormed off toward the bathroom.

"Again?" she called after him. "Right now?"

"What? You want some?" He threw a knowing smirk at Dee.

She shook her head and he disappeared into the bathroom.

Dee stared at me, vexed. I thought we shared a storm, but I guess that didn't matter here. I wasn't her blood.

I imagined my pops sliding through the front door and freezing the room. People would look at him and he'd come throw his paw on my head a little too strong 'cause he didn't know any better. People would think, *Damn, that's a big nigga! Big. Big.* And I'd smile 'cause I knew what they were thinking. He'd slap Dee's ass again and tell her to wait in the car. Then I'd tell him the quote I wanted and he'd say, Man, G, that's real cold. Keep your head in them books. I'd smile again, the biggest one, from my gut, because I was going to write our history—history of our pride, lions of blackness in all our shades. I pulled my shirt off, my skin cold even in the dead of August.

No one burst through the door. I ended up getting a tattoo of Jesus walking on water, just the outline, with light shading, after an Alexander Ivanov painting I'd seen online once. It took Mando three hours and it hurt like hell and I wanted to cry because the needle felt like it was scraping through my ribs, but he just kept moving. Even though he had glassy eyes and seemed to tweak a lot, his fingers stayed steady, and then he was done.

WHEN WE GOT back home, Pops was in the kitchen eating cold pizza. He was going to work in a few hours, but I asked him if he wanted to play ball anyway. He said he was tired and I told him I knew he couldn't dunk. He just kept eating.

"I got a tattoo today," I said.

"Oh yeah?"

I lifted my gray shirt, which was stained black on the inside from the ink, and showed him the art going from my chest down to my ribs.

He opened up the fridge, took out some fruit punch, and drank it straight from the bottle. "Keep it Christian," he said, and laughed, and that was it.

I called my mom and told her. She cried for a long time. *Why'd you ruin your beautiful body?* she asked. *Why'd you mar yourself?* Then she cried a while longer and told me to move out here if I loved it so much, and I said I would, Pops would be happy to have me. We stayed on the phone for a bit in silence. Her breathing finally calmed down and she said she loved me and hung up.

THE NEXT MORNING, I woke up to yelling from their bedroom. "You took him to that crackhead!"

"Shut up, Lonnie. He's not a fuckin' crackhead."

"Deandra, niggas who smoke crack are crackheads."

"You would know," Dee said.

I never knew my pops to raise his hand to a woman, but I heard something break. There was some more shouting and then the garage door opened. I lay awake on the air mattress until the sun broke through the brown blinds on the window and spilled out across the white sheets. Some manila folders had fell from one of the storage boxes next to the bed. I pushed them off my sheets, rolled to face the wall, and waited until I heard the peace of bacon frying. It was Saturday. Pops left again and came back around midday with bagged eyes, smelling like hot-dog water instead of bleach. He took a long cloudy look at me, then looked away and went into his room before I could say anything. I waited up as late as I could that night for him to wake up. I fell asleep to the sounds of summer-league basketball coming from the TV in the other room.

*　　*　　*

LEAH CAME DURING my junior year of college. The girls before her faded and I started again at one.

July was hot in Ithaca, and the heat came in damp from storm clouds, turning my dorm room into a sauna. Leah sat on the edge of my bed. We were fresh from a cold shower and already starting to sweat. I sprawled on my back letting the last few drops of water air-dry. Her eyes scanned the room like a mother's eyes. Her brown hair hung wet and clean down to the middle of her back. As I got up, she asked where I was going. I gotta work, I said. As part of the scholarship, I had to coach basketball camp for at-risk kids in Ithaca. Aw, my baby giving back, she said. I pulled on a pair of basketball shorts. Gotta sing for my supper, I said. Stop complaining, she said, brushing some crumbs off the corner of my mattress, her hands pale against the maroon. And change your sheets, she said, then smoothed the edges tight and flat. She liked to smooth and fix and make things neat, molding with her narrow fingers calm and knowing, the look in her eyes gentle—*Let me help build you.* She lay down and patted the bed next to her. I pressed into her and she draped an arm across my stomach. Her limbs were long and smelled like soap, the soft-scented bar kind, not the mango-cocktail gel shit.

I had to go soon but didn't want to move just yet. She traced her red nails around my tattoo, her hair heavy and warm across my collarbone. Her fingers moved along the outline of His robes, and I asked, Why'd your people kill Him?

She smiled with her deep brown eyes and kissed my chest, where His head was engraved. 'Cause it made for a good story, she said. She licked up to my nipple and I pushed her head away. I didn't know you were even religious, she said.

I'm not, really, I started. It's mostly my pops' side. They all sing in the choir and do the Gospel thing. My pops had two choices—preacher or ballplayer.

She moved her face up till her lips rested in that soft spot below my jaw. The spot that made me want to taste her. I'm sure he had more than two, she said.

I didn't feel like putting her onto my history so I was silent.

She looked across the room at a picture of my pops in his NFL uniform. I guess he made the right choice, she said.

It'd been almost five years since I'd seen him last. My mom said he wasn't the same. More than his body had been banged up. I thought about the shadow-quick phone calls. I hadn't heard much from Dee or Whit either. No one wanted to speak on it. Somehow, not naming Pops' troubles kept them minor.

Yeah, I told Leah. I couldn't put his unraveling on the NFL like my mom did.

He's huge, Leah said.

And I'm not? I said.

Not that big, you're not, she said.

I pretended to bite her nose and she scrunched her whole face up.

When she left that day, I watched her from my fifth-story window, watched her stride away to her business as the wind from the coming rain shook the maple leaves and obscured her image. I watched her walk up Highland Ave. as long as I could, until she bent around the corner and I lost sight.

LEAH WANTED TO meet my parents. My mom would have loved her because she could only glance at women, at people in general, always confusing security for a life fulfilled. I think the trauma of the divorce and Koreatown was still with her. After Saba's parents and a few others', Leah's mom and dad would've looked like salvation. They were both professors out in Denver and would've signaled peace where there was none, at least not in my vision. When I'd visited, her parents had a group of PhD students over for dinner, and her mother let her eyes linger too long on a couple of the young men, made comments about what we were wearing, asked me how tall I was, said she loved the basketball build, then got dreamy like she wanted a night away, or maybe a few, from the life she'd made. But then she'd go back to talking about the politics of cleft states, and everything returned to normal. Leah's dad looked at me a few times like he might've caught it too, and then after dinner I heard her parents whisper-fighting in the den. I kept my ear open to the lessons—hoping history wouldn't repeat itself.

Leah's eyes wandered just like her mom's. When I'd call her on it, she'd say, *Aw, you're jealous,* or *Relax, tiger,* and I imagined she'd learned how to manage men from her mother too. My mom had gone on loving my pops every day for fourteen years since the split, without cease. At least that's what she claimed. I guess she was romantic like that, but it's always easier to love a memory.

One time, at her place, after I rolled her out, Leah sat on my ass, leaned her forearms on my back and blew on my neck. I didn't mind cuddling in her bedroom. It had pastel-colored paintings and scented candles, shit that gave you a cuddly feel.

Stop, I said.

She put her face down next to mine. You know you like it, she said.

Why don't you give me a back rub? I said.

Who do I look like? she said. You should give me one.

Girl, I'll rub every inch of you, I said.

She laughed and rolled off me. Go ahead.

I started up at the base of her skull, real gentle with just one hand. Then I kissed in between her shoulder blades and started kissing her sides and hips.

Really? she said. That's as far as you're going to make it?

I flipped her over real quick and started biting her stomach. My teeth marks were bright red in the flesh next to her hipbones.

Stop, stop.

I looked up at her.

Come here, she said. She tossed the hair off her shoulder and I laid my head there. Are you going to let me meet your parents soon?

Damn, I said, you *really* didn't want to fuck again, huh?

She rolled her eyes at me. You've met mine, she said.

Wandering eyes aside, they had seemed to sparkle in their suburban home near Denver. Truth be told, I imagined it was a lot like the California suburb I'd been born in while my pops still played, before the 49ers did him dirty. Leah's family had a fire pit out back and the whole family did dishes, synchronized like they were running a motion offense. Then we all sat and watched late-night television. Shit, even though they were Jewish, I could almost envision them caroling together.

And? I said.

And I want to meet them, she said. They won't scare me away.

That's not what I'm worried about, I lied, and I went down to kiss her inner thighs. She closed her knees and I rested my head there, gazing at her. She laughed and pinched her face up the cute way she always did. Put your glasses on, I told her.

Let me meet your parents.

FINE, I SAID, and spread her legs. Now put your glasses on.

The moonlight that shone through her lace curtains was pretty on her skin. Her hair was sprawled on the pillow next to where I'd been beside her. I wanted to lie back down and smell her hair again. I wanted to fog her glasses and kiss her thighs and I really did want her to meet both my parents. Our kids would be little JAPs with traces of nigga in them and have soft hair and beautiful eyes and smiles.

I didn't ever talk about my family. All she knew were the pictures in my dorm. I even had a few from when I was little, when we were still all together. Maybe she made assumptions about my folks because her parents had worked so hard on their love, like homemade-chocolate-covered-strawberries type love, like surprise-love-poem type love, like Marvin Gaye/vibrator/Jacuzzi-session type love. But I knew the small fractures in her parents' bond even if she didn't want to see or hear them.

That night, after she fell asleep, I packed up my overnight bag, got in my car, and left. I drove along the shore of Cayuga for a while, heading nowhere, with the image of her sleeping sound stuck like hooks in me. The lake was much prettier at night. I parked by the falls in the state park and picked out some town lights across the way.

It would be three hours earlier in Washington. I hadn't heard from my pops since I graduated high school, but I tried the numbers I had anyway, once on his cell and once at home.

Dee picked up and told me he hadn't been around in months. The world felt on loop.

"He isn't picking up his cell," I said.

"New number," she said.

"How's Whit?"

She sighed deep like she had a story. "She's asleep already."

"He still come around?"

She coughed. "Some things you gotta ask him yourself," she said.

I asked for the new number.

"Hold on." Her voice sounded a thousand packs worse and crackled through the earpiece. She gave me the new number and hung up. I called three times and each time a man picked up and said he didn't know a Lonnie. Stop calling.

A FEW DAYS after I'd gotten my tattoo, Pops said we were going to Burlington Coat Factory to get me jazzed up, but before we even hit the highway, I saw my bags in the backseat. He was taking me to the airport a week early. It was like something was all used up, like we had stopped building together all of a sudden. That was the worst of it. Even then I wondered if we'd ever start again. My ribs still hurt like hell as we walked through the totem poles of the Sea-Tac Airport in silence. They stretched up, towering over him. Faces like legacies carved into trees that had once jutted up into the blue northwest sky, preservations of family histories, legends incarnate. I loved that word. The word was big enough to fill the universe—legend of the sun and moon and stars. Family legends, so many lost.

We were late and his strides were long. I had to trot to keep up.

"C'mon, G," he said. I bumped into people as we went, my eyes fixed on those etched histories. "Gio!" he said.

"I can get it removed," I said.

My face got hot. I tried to stop but he grabbed my wrist and yanked me through the crowd.

"Dee told me to get it," I said. "I just wanted a quote."

"It's not about the damn tattoo."

I saw a fast-food Chinese restaurant and thought it was my last hope. "Can we get some food? I'm hungry."

He eyed the Panda Express, then checked his watch. We stood still and silent for a moment. He was probably thinking about egg rolls and lo mein and thinking about them hard. But then he started to drag me toward the gate again.

I must've asked why a dozen times. He kept yanking my arm until my shoulder hurt almost as much as my ribs.

"You have to go home," he said.

Home hit me like a fist and I stopped asking.

When we got to the check-in, he confirmed the ticket change. The attendant said I'd be able to get on. He smiled at her and there was a little fear that crept behind her green eyes. It was some of the prettiest green I'd ever seen. He saw the fear too so he said, "Thank ya kindly." Then she smiled back. My pops knew how to turn the black folk on when he wanted too.

He gave me five dollars to get some food during my layover in Chicago. I wanted to tell him that I knew, just like the ticket, it was my mom's money. Instead, I hugged him good-bye. I could feel the sweat beginning to soak through his green shirt.

There are pictures in my mom's house of them on vacation in San Diego. His shirts hang like dresses down past her knees. She looks happy in those pics. They both do. He is a happy ghost in those pictures. A happy black ghost with my smile.

* * *

By the end of that summer before I returned for my senior year, Leah had quit calling. When I didn't respond to her messages, the texts and e-mails stopped too. My pops hadn't resurfaced. Dee and my mom had been bitching at each other about it on the phone for weeks. I wanted to call Leah every day, apologize, tell her what was up, but it was unfair to leave her with two options—pity or bullshit.

I was back at my mom's, eating soup and watching the light change through the window. Fall was coming. The sun was crisper and not hazy like the shimmering heat of summer. My mom and I looked at each other across the kitchen table, in silence. When the home phone rang, somehow we both knew.

She answered it. Her voice was hushed. "Yes, he's home. Lonnie, he's been calling you and he—" Her voice was rising and he must've cut her off. "Yes, I'll put him on." She walked over to me with eyes so full they would have burst if I hadn't smiled and slouched back in my chair.

"Soup's good," I said.

"It's your father."

"I'm not here right now." But she looked like she would crack again so I took the phone. "Ayo, Pops."

"What's up, G-Money? Heard you tried to call me a while back."

"Yeah, glad to hear you livin'." He wheezed into the phone and I felt bad. "You been running?" I asked.

"What?" he said.

"Never mind."

"I was calling to check up on you," he said.

"Ray," someone yelled in the background on his end. "Ray!"

He muffled the phone and said something to the dude yelling.

44

"What's going on?" I asked.

"G, lemme call you right back."

"Yeah," I said, but there was already a dial tone. I looked at my mom. "It'll be in May. I'll give you the date when I know," I said. "That sounds real nice."

The operator's voice began to play and I hung up.

A few years later, my cousin finally told me he'd been staying in a funky spot down in Rainier Vista. He didn't use his real name around the folks he was staying with. The fat nigga had gotten Ray off a bottle of Sweet Baby Ray's barbecue sauce so that's what he went by. Ray "Lion" Campbell didn't have the same ring, though. I didn't know if he was working or what he was doing. He didn't even check up on Whitney anymore.

BE GOOD TO ME

Tayla and Rolls first met during one of the summer Portuguese feasts in East Providence. She spent a long time just looking at him before trying to be seen. He was standing around an open fire with a cup of red wine and a cup of seasoning to toss over a five-dollar skewer of roasting beef. Even though the cups were plastic and he had Air Forces on his feet, his face looked serious in the light, like he'd built the fire himself and aimed to keep it burning for a thousand years. She left her friends and posted nearby, trying to catch his glance. She was glad she'd worn the powder-blue sundress her older sister, Candace, said made her look refined.

An hour later they were on the steps of St. Francis Xavier and he had opened the sketch pad he always traveled with. She looked young, and he drew a caricature of her with a preacher's robe and a lollipop.

When she asked about it, he said, "You're so sweet and wholesome, I'ma call you Christ's candy."

It was weak game and she rolled her eyes. "I don't believe in God," she said. He paused and she quickly added, "At least not in the church sense."

He launched into the problems with religious institutions, noted the value of communal worship, all in student-speak. He would be a sophomore at college come fall, and his boys would've been too if things had turned out different. She listened for a while before she asked why he was religious. He deflected, asked her where she went to school. She thought about lying but said she'd be a junior at Lincoln High in the fall.

That made him quiet.

"Don't be weird," she said.

Rolls looked at her face in the dim orange light from the church and started drawing again. He said he was religious because he needed a compass. "It's like a North Star," he said. "People talk themselves out of doing good too often."

She wanted to lean in for a kiss, but Candace's voice played loudly—*Fast women are worth less than fast food*. Rolls flipped the page of his notebook and sketched some more.

"You look really pretty when you smile," he said.

She studied his profile for a second before reaching out a little too quick, turning his face, and kissing him close-mouthed. "I'm not as wholesome as you think," she said.

After that, Rolls started picking her up in secret—secret from her parents and his pops. He told his boys, but they all said she was a myth and asked why he hadn't brought her around. Rolls joked, but not without pride, about how he had to pull up past her house so her pops wouldn't wake up. But they all knew that strict parents didn't always make for good girls and loose parents didn't always make for loose ones. Rolls liked that she wore dresses, not low-riding jeans with Js. Still, he hadn't introduced her to his father. The rules would change once he did.

Tayla liked that he took her around to places alive with noise or places where time seemed to stretch. She liked that Rolls cared about more than just sports and pussy. Though she knew that was probably on his mind too. The way he spoke seemed so composed, like he'd written it out first. Sometimes he'd lower the volume on a song just to tell her the history of the sample that was in it. She'd tell him he was a weirdo and turn the music back up, but she was impressed. She liked the feeling of drifting around with him.

Still, she was mad that he never introduced her to his boys. She asked why he didn't take her to Dub's parties since he talked about them so much. He told her that she wouldn't like them. Finally, one day, he said that she didn't belong there.

She looked out the passenger window for a minute. "I can take care of myself," she said.

The following Saturday, Rolls brought Tayla to Dub's. She drew attention but hardly made a sound. That was her youth.

Rolls leaned against a boxy, flat-screen TV, one leg crossed in front of the other. She didn't get tired of taking in the angles of his wiry body. Tight brown pants accented his frame. His face was dark and fine-featured like none she'd ever seen before. He told her that way back, his people were Italian-Ethiopian. He descended from kings.

Nigga, everybody can't be king, his boys'd say. It don't make sense. Some motherfuckers gotta be average. When they really wanted to fuck with him, they'd start calling him Selassie—*Your sneakers are trashed, Selassie. Roll another J, Selassie. How much you got on this pizza, Selassie?*

Tayla watched him shift his weight with an ease and lightness. He was the paranoid type, but she didn't see it that way. She thought it was just artistic energy, something he was bursting with. When they were alone, his thoughts wandered and he'd sketch and draw. Sometimes he talked while he drew, like he was narrating his art to her.

At the party, he and Dub spoke fast. They were all tipsy and the words flew by her into the kitchen. She lost the thread of their conversation somewhere around moral imperatives and never quite picked it back up.

"Don't give me that 'It's all relative' bullshit," Rolls said. "Some niggas are just heinous."

"And I bet you think you're not," Dub said. He looked down at Tayla sitting on the plastic folding chair.

She fixed her skirt and recrossed her legs. The chair creaked beneath her and she glanced at Rolls. He reached down and rested his hand on the back of her neck.

"So healthy." He broke into a smile that could pacify a lion.

She tucked a spiral of hair back behind her ear. The room was empty—just plastic folding chairs, the TV, and a rug that was still rolled up in the corner. Only a couple stragglers remained. It hadn't been one of Dub's best parties.

It was his mom's place. The party was always there. His mom worked the late shift at Walmart and that left the good hours open for getting down. The space was mostly empty but somehow still cramped. It was on the top floor of a three-family home and was packed to the gills whenever Gio and Rolls bought liquor or whenever somebody came across a cheap bootlegger selling "imported" aguardiente, which meant it had been brewed in a garbage can, and decided to be generous with it.

When Rolls and Tayla got back to her neighborhood after Dub's, she touched his knee and said to drive past her street. He looked over at her and she thought he might smile, or kiss her, or ask if she was sure, but he just continued on until they reached the small river with its dirt parking lot that fit only two cars. He cut the engine. The dashboard lights still shone green for a minute. She took in his features once more and knew how good his lips would feel on hers. In the past weeks, they'd fooled around and she'd left him hard. She liked that power. Her mom had told her never to use sex to manipulate a man, but Candace told her that any man worth shit would wait. Her friends told her different.

The car lights went completely dark. The trees and clouded night made the inside an inkwell, too murky to see him clearly any longer, but she knew he was slouched back in the driver's seat like usual, leaning so far you could barely see his head through the driver's-side window. The car sighed and clicked as it cooled. She wanted to ask more about what he and Dub had been talking about earlier. She hadn't studied philosophy. Really, she just liked the quality of Rolls' voice when he got excited about something. It was like listening to her mom talk about piano. His voice would come out so loud and assured.

Before she could speak, his hand was between her thighs. His touch was cool, skin thick. She squeezed her legs tighter but didn't remove his hand. His breath on her ear tickled. She leaned away a little, then his lips were below her jaw, his teeth gently on the soft part of her neck. He paused a second and blew cool air where he'd been kissing. Chills went up her arms. She held his head, felt the coarseness of his hair beneath her fingers. He took his hand away and unbuttoned his jeans.

Headlights passed and for a moment she saw his outline—he was already hard. Her friends had told her it was easy, that all boys get so amped they'll say you're the best in the world.

He propped it up and grabbed the back of her head. Her body caught on the seat belt.

"Hey," she said, and stiffened. Her eyes were adjusted now and his smile was dimmed in the dark.

"My bad," he said. He undid her seat belt and kissed her again. His lips were gentle, then her head was being forced down over the console again. The gearshift was hard in her stomach. She stopped to turn her body. He put the seat all the way down and pulled her by the back of the head. She coughed a bit.

"That's it," he said.

She sucked it like the top of a Popsicle, but it was too wide. She looked through the dark at what she thought was his face.

"Are you, like, huge?" she asked.

"I'm happy with it." He laughed, then grabbed the back of her head again. Something about his laugh relaxed her and this time she was able to get her mouth farther down. She used her hand to brace against the seat. Eventually she eased, but time moved slowly. Her jaw started to ache. He draped one arm over her back and slid his fingers beneath her waistband till they reached the top of her ass. She noticed her own wetness for the first time that night. Then he grabbed a handful of her hair and thrust himself into her mouth harder. She gagged but he thrust harder till she thought she was choking and tried to pull away.

"Breathe through your nose," he said. "Be a good girl."

Snot bubbled in her throat and nose. Still, she kept on and squeezed her eyes shut and thought of how he'd called her beautiful when he caught her fixing the bunches in her dresses and skirts, how gentle his lips were moments ago, his faraway eyes when he drew.

One hand rested gently on her shoulder, the other still had a fistful of her hair. She couldn't move. She was going to throw up, then her throat and mouth filled. She felt force on her head for a long time while she labored to swallow. When his grip released, she sat up quickly to ease the pressure from the console, sniffled, and swallowed again. The taste was unexpectedly bitter, almost citrus. Her throat hurt. She pinched his side hard. He laughed again. She felt stupid, younger than she wanted to be. Her eyes still watered as he drove her home, but she kept them locked on him, staring the way her mom did when she wanted to burn a hole in her father. She looked for something new that she hadn't seen before. She wanted to ask if he'd done that a lot. Really she wanted to know if that's how it always was. The speed and force felt unlike him.

When she opened the door to go, the car lights came on and she searched his face. She wasn't dumb enough to say he made her feel "special," but she also thought she was more than a piece of ass to him. He listened when she spoke. He had things to say other than *Tayla has DSL*—which she'd seen written on desks after she made out with Max Gillette on a staircase in eighth grade. Max was a punk. She'd cussed him out, but that didn't stop him and his friends from talking. Candace said that's all boys could talk about and that the more they talked about it, the less they got.

Rolls' eyes were low but steadied on her face like she was his sketch pad. He was searching too. He reached out and touched her shoulder. She shrugged his hand away. But he moved his hand up to her face and rubbed her lips gently with the edge of his thumb. He looked about five minutes away from sleep. She kept her face stiff and said nothing. When his car was gone, she tried to trace her own lips, prodding them to see how they really felt.

Rolls got a lot of shit because Tayla was still in high school. But really he caught shade because she was thick in the way that drove men ragged, and his boys were slumping. He caught shade because she was light-skinned in the way that black actresses are always two tones lighter than the men they're paired with. He caught shade because she had the kind of lips that could suck the brown off and his boys got fuzzy-headed when they looked at her. Slumps are a motherfucker. So when he bragged about getting dome, they told him it didn't count if he didn't pipe.

After that first night, she didn't return his calls for a week, but he knew she'd enjoyed it somewhere deep down. He'd felt it with his own hand. He also knew the women at college would crucify him for thinking that way, though they'd ask for the same treatment behind closed doors. The same women he'd been in photography class with. The ones who said his photos "told stories."

His scholarship allowed him to meet a lot of people who talked about art, some inspiring, some full of shit. The things he'd picked up working in his father's camera shop down by the Benny's on Central had taken him a long way. The shop sold old Nikons and Canons and developed pictures taken on similarly old machines. They had a good core of loyal customers. Most of the day, when his dad wasn't fixing cameras or trying to make sales, he sat back in his plush leather chair in his office flipping through books of Ansel Adams and Gordon Parks. Rolls worked in the darkroom all day and left his phone behind the cash register. His dad was an older man, gnarled and wiry, who'd cycled through marriages. Rolls was from his third, the one that'd stuck long enough to make a kid, though his mom had ridden into the sunset with a pretty boy from Denver who made her feel "new." That all happened before Rolls turned one.

He and his pops never talked much about anything except which safelights matched which types of paper and the different lenses to use based on the camera's sensor size, but he didn't mind. It was their shared language. He wondered if his pops had talked more before the split but never asked.

Rolls liked the 35mm lenses that made the world a little wider. He liked looking at photos with stories near the edges. He had taken a wide shot of a white woman walking down Broadway. On the left edge, a man is clapping his hands, hunched over, staring at her ass but with an insane expression. He loved that one because of the philosophy, not that ass rules the planet, but that most of the world exists outside our perception. Though on his worst days he also might've thought the former. He liked expansive movies too—Westerns, just like his dad. Sometimes they talked movies, but never women. His dad thought since he couldn't hold his own relationships together, he had no place to offer wisdom. Still, Rolls was thankful for the words they did share. His boys knew a lot worse.

ON A FRIDAY in mid-July, after a week of ignored phone calls, he figured Tayla might open up. He didn't know if he missed her. His niggas would just say that the thirst is real. That explanation seemed simpler. Back home, the thirst was understood. He understood it at school too. He just didn't speak on it.

On his lunch break, he hit Tayla up with a text. After work, he read her reply: *Pick me up after 10. Britt's coming.* Britt had a mole on her cheek the size of a Hershey's Kiss, and a part between her front teeth. But if that's what it took to see Tayla again, he was down.

TAYLA SAT IN the back of the car with Britt.

"I like this track," Tayla said.

"You don't know Barrington Levy," he said.

"You don't know me," she said, and smiled.

Rolls turned up the CD and pulled out of the neighborhood. He was already scheming on how to get rid of Britt. The girls at school would call him sexist. He remembered trying to tell Rye that when he called his car a good girl, he was making a gendered statement. Rye'd looked at him like he'd just shit out his mouth and said that if Rolls was gay he could just tell him. Rolls dropped it.

As they whispered in the back, he thought about the sorority girls at Trinity on the nights they went out, tight black dresses like a second layer of skin, flooding frat house living rooms. He felt whiplash.

When he pulled up to the party, Dub was on the bottom-floor porch burning the last bit of a spliff. His neighbors bummed weed off him sometimes when they were desperate, and, in exchange, Dub had free run of their porch and caught no complaints when nights got wild.

"Ladies, it's all upstairs," he said. He waved with his off hand to the stairs on the side of the house.

The girls looked at Rolls.

"It's just a party," he said.

"We'll be right with you," Dub said, trying to sound smooth.

The girls went through the door and disappeared and Rolls took the roach from Dub to pull the last hit.

"Nigga, you gotta stop bringing jailbait to my house," Dub said. "Who the fuck is Skidmark Sally?"

Rolls coughed out smoke with a laugh and then threw the roach. "She's Tayla's friend. It was the only way she'd come."

"You strung out over some high school chick?" Dub said.

"Fuck outta here." Rolls turned to head up.

"Wait, wait, wait." Rolls stopped. "You hit yet?" Dub asked.

Rolls continued to the door.

"I worry about you sometimes," Dub said. "Little Rakim, falling in love." Rolls didn't give him the satisfaction of turning back again. "I bet you taking her out for fancy dinners and writing her poems and shit too."

Upstairs the place was packed. It was small on the top floor, slanted ceilings and people bunched in corners. The only light came from above the stove. A cooler of jungle juice sat on the half wall that separated the tiny kitchen from the dance floor, which was just an unfurnished living room. People mobbed around the cooler, making it hard to move anywhere. Dub let his inner circle into his room to smoke with a towel under the door and the window open, usually just the many women he wanted to get with and never would. Dub was the type to try and leverage situations, had been that way since middle school, and everyone made a show of dapping him up or telling him the party was live. But Dub was too busy checking up on the women who hadn't told him off yet. Either that or he was keeping folks from fighting, which was tough because the liquor was stocked, the place was hot, and too many dudes were getting no play. Rolls posted on the edge of the dance floor and talked with Rye and Gio and a few other people while he clocked Dub's work ethic. Girls came and went trying to get at Rye, the only one who was actually wifed up. The cooler slowly emptied.

Tayla and Britt stood together just outside Rolls' circle of friends, laughing and talking with people he knew. Men came in a steady stream at Tayla and checked her all the way down to the turquoise heels that matched her skirt, which made her skin glow. The party was so hot, people's hair stuck to their foreheads. Tayla's spirals began to droop in the humidity.

Someone Rolls didn't know eventually cut between the two girls and his boys and leaned real close to whisper in Tayla's ear. She threw her head back in easy laughter, a gesture Rolls had seen on her before when he cracked jokes. The next moment Rolls had his arms around her waist. Then Dub and Gio were next to him. Gio pulled Britt back into the mix and Dub looked the kid up and down.

"You're my li'l bro's friend, right?" Dub said to him.

The kid sucked his teeth. "You know me, man."

"Yeah. That cooler's running out quick." Dub pointed into the kitchen.

The kid glanced at the mass of people behind him, then back at Dub. He turned to leave.

"My bro's always inviting trouble," Dub said.

With his arms still around Tayla's waist, Rolls told her that he wanted to dance.

She nodded at the dance floor. "I can't dance like that." Someone'd brought a cheap multicolored disco light that threw spots of pink and green on the bodies as they moved in the darkness.

"Yes you can," Rolls said.

She tried to face him, but he held his grip around her waist.

"Pretend you're all alone at home," he said. He kissed her on the back of her head through a mass of hair.

"I'm not going to leave Britt," she said. She broke free and dragged her friend over.

Rolls turned to Dub. "Dance with Britt."

"Uh, I got a bum-ass knee," he said. Britt's face looked pinched.

Rolls reached an arm out and pulled Dub over. They huddled. "C'mon, nigga, sacrifice makes the heart stronger," he said, patting on his chest.

"Fuck that confused-ass Confucius shit."

Rolls glanced back at Britt and Tayla to see if they'd heard. Britt was pretending to be busy, moving her hips and surveying the packed room, and Tayla looked impatient.

"Help me out," Rolls said.

The music swelled and the noise shook the place like the inside of a bass speaker.

Dub grabbed Gio and forced him into the huddle. "Ask G. He's a sensitive college boy too."

"Ask me what?" Gio said.

"Dance with Britt?" Rolls said.

Gio glanced behind at Tayla and Britt, who was getting animated, trying to leave, probably, saying the party was wack and all the other lame-ass things people say when they're getting no love.

"My brother." Rolls smiled like a Bible salesman.

"Fuck," Gio said. He turned and took Britt onto the dance floor.

Dancehall came on the speakers and everybody lost it. Tayla's body moved stiff in Rolls' hands. He felt from her stomach to the meat of her thighs and let his hands stay there, rubbing her down. They swayed together, gently at first. Tayla's body eased into the rhythm, the way Rolls imagined she moved when no one was watching. He grabbed her waist and started to thrust light. Tayla tilted her head back and grinded herself into him. Then as the drums of the song picked up, she bent forward and became a new person all at once, arching her back and swinging herself into Rolls with the heart of the song. She felt him rise to attention and liked the pressure, wanted to show him that she could get down, was down. He started stroking like he was hitting it from behind, like he was trying to bruise something, and she knew she was driving him wild, his hands all over her shoulders, down to her hips and ass. When he lifted one of her legs, she lost the rhythm for a second and he realized he had broken the trance. He kept moving with the beat, but they'd lost it. He tried to push through the awkwardness. She flailed a little with her leg and he held her tight so she didn't lose her balance. The song switched and Rolls looked around the cramped room. Gio was trying not to make eye contact with Britt, who was smiling all thirsty. Rolls wanted to dance another song but Tayla said no. The spotted lights kept blinking at shutter speed.

JUST BEFORE DAWN, only Dub, Gio, Rolls, and the two girls were left. Rye had gone home to his girl. Dub poured the rest of the juice from the cooler into cups, only about a sip for everyone.

The girls picked up dirty cups and Rolls said to put them down. "I wouldn't fuck with those," he said.

"Let them experiment," Dub said. He made his way around the small apartment with a giant trash bag.

Rolls poured his drink into Gio's. "I'm headed out. They gotta get home before the sun comes up."

"Help me clean first," Dub said.

"We funded this shit," Rolls said.

"So? It's my house."

"Your mom's house," Gio said.

Dub stopped cleaning and stood up straight. Gio shot him a look to see where Dub was gonna take it. Tayla finished her drink, leaned on Rolls.

"I gotta piss," Rolls said.

Tayla let her head lean back and her hair hung like Spanish moss. Dub looked Gio dead in the eye and handed him the bag. He followed Rolls down the small hallway. He was inside and shutting the bathroom door before Rolls had even unbuttoned his pants.

"What you want?" Rolls said.

"Those girls are ready."

Rolls turned away from the toilet, his belt still undone, and stared at Dub with tight eyes.

"Look, either you can get pussy, or we can all get some," Dub said.

"You bitched at me for bringing young girls and now you want in?" Rolls tried to imagine a girl from Trinity at Dub's that night. How things would've gone down.

"You love her," Dub said. "Don't you?"

Rolls cocked his head at Dub. "Don't talk crazy."

Dub just waited for more explanation.

Rolls' mind flashed through the scenes, coming slowly to resolution—the dimness of the empty living room, their five figures dark and twisting, the dawn not yet strong enough to chase them out. For all he knew, they might be down. Rolls took out his phone. It was just after four. He tried bringing up Dub's girl. "What about Mone?"

"Don't play that. This shit don't count," Dub said.

Rolls didn't know how it would go. The whole frame was muddy. He imagined Dub on Tayla. "Nah, man," he said.

"Don't be a bitch."

"Seconds, nigga?" Rolls said. "Really?"

Dub cut his eyes at him.

"You want to see my dick that bad?" Rolls unzipped his pants.

"Pause," Dub said, and held his hand up. "Look, if that's wifey, just say it."

For a long while, the drip of the faucet was the only sound.

Dub smirked. "Those college bunnies got you weak in the knees."

The white-yellow light made the shower curtain and the beige paint around the mirror look dirty even though Rolls knew Dub's mom washed it down every Saturday.

There was a knock on the bathroom door. "I'll piss outside," Rolls said. As he walked out past Dub, he yelled Britt's name. She came quick. He grabbed Tayla by the arm and she tried to jerk free on the way out.

"I worry about you sometimes," Dub said. His voice echoed in the narrow staircase, cramped enough that you almost had to crawl out.

AFTER HE DROPPED Britt off, Rolls headed back down by the river with Tayla. He tried to get her in the backseat and when she said no, he was rougher than their first night. Again he could feel her wetness. He even stuck his thumb in her and she gasped but then pushed his hand away. She made him slow down and convinced herself that was the real him, taking his time, being attentive with her. She couldn't lie, she wanted it in the backseat too, but not yet, not this easy. She'd seen how the fast girls got treated—passed around. Her mom said it was a damn shame they didn't know their own worth.

After he came, he drove her home. It was a nice neighborhood with trees and lawns and space. He pulled far enough down the street that her house wasn't in sight and parked, left the engine running. The sky was dangerously light, penetrating the corners of the dark world. Her face was softly lit by purple sky. He wondered if she knew the things that were moving on the edge of the frame—hungry, hunting for a face like hers.

"What do your friends think of me?" she asked.

He waited too long. "Baby," he said, trying to play it off, "they think the world of you."

She looked ahead silent and stone-faced. He wanted to tell her they thought she was a dime, but that wouldn't be good enough, and the truth, that they thought he should pipe and quit, definitely wouldn't cut it. Especially since he was desperate to convince himself the same shit. He took a deep breath.

"Do you believe in good and evil?" he asked.

"What?" She slumped back in her seat. "Why?"

"I don't know. Fuck it. Forget it."

"No, what do you mean?"

"It's late."

"Stop trying to get rid of me," she said.

The birds called an alarm into the morning. Rolls leaned back into his seat and closed his eyes. He started to talk slowly about pure reason and practical reason. He tried to break down Kant, first saying he was German and Germans are crazy and depressing so she shouldn't feel bad if she didn't get it. Truthfully, he'd barely understood the concept himself. He explained that the universal was already in motion every time you made a decision. "It's not so much do unto others as you would want others to do unto you," he said. "It's more like do unto others as you would want everyone in the universe to do unto each other." He started to mumble a little bit, falling asleep. He turned his head to look at her.

She stared directly at him. She actually cared. Back in high school, he used to tell his boys he skipped English class instead of admitting he was in the honors class.

"I get it," she said.

"Yeah?"

"Yeah, good exists and wrong exists outside—they just exist. It's not like it changes case to case."

He wanted to make the world safer for her and knew that admitting as much was foolish.

"Yeah," she said. "Like if something is wrong once, it's wrong every other time."

A knock shook the car. "Get out!" A man's voice.

Rolls leaped out of himself before he turned to the noise, right outside his door.

"Get out!" the man said again.

Tayla opened the door quick and was into the morning. Rolls quickly locked the door after it shut.

"Open it!"

"Dad, stop!" Tayla yelled.

Her father banged the driver's-side door and pulled at the handle.

"Get in the house!"

"Dad, don't!"

He banged his fist again. "Get the fuck out!"

Rolls knew how that convo would go and he didn't feel like throwing hands with a forty-something-year-old. It was five fifteen a.m., too early for that shit. Plus, when her dad banged on the window, Rolls noticed how meaty the fucker's fists were. His boys would never let him live it down if he got knocked out over this girl.

Rolls looked into her father's eyes, inches away, kept staring. Her father probably knew because he'd done the same shit years ago. He jerked at the handle and the plastic lever snapped free. Rolls flinched and scrambled to put the car in drive. He eased off, giving her dad time to back away from the car. The man spun and kicked the door with the heel of his sneaker. The move was smooth—made Rolls think it was a good play staying in the car.

"If I see you again, I'll break your fucking jaw!"

When he was ten yards past, Rolls slowed and opened his window. His half-drunk pride got the best of him and he stuck his head out the window to say something, sobered up a bit in the cool morning air, and just spat instead.

THE ONLY OTHER time Tayla had ever been grounded was when she walked down to the Blackstone alone at ten years old. Her dad said he'd grounded her so she would learn right from wrong. He said he'd grounded her because she knew better. Her mom had said they only wanted to keep her safe. Her mom took away her for fun books because she liked to read more than watch TV.

This time she didn't feel like she was being kept safe. She

enjoyed spending time with Rolls. He had corny lines—they all did—but his mind would switch over and he would talk to her for hours about things unrelated to her eyes or lips or body. She didn't think about bringing him home, not after that night, anyway, but she thought Candace would've liked him.

She spent her punishment around the house reading Jane Austen or one of the other boring dead authors assigned to her for summer reading. She wanted to ask Rolls what to read. In between time, she volunteered at the Boys and Girls Club, which she liked because the kids were cute and rambunctious. On days when she felt the urge to drift, she'd lay out by her neighbor's pool in the hot August sun pretending she didn't need sunblock. Her parents hadn't taken her phone, so she texted Rolls nonstop. A lot of *Sorry, my dad is a lunatic* texts.

While she was grounded, at the beginning of August, Rolls sent a package using Britt's name. Her parents gave it to her without question. The frame was dark wood, inside—a watercolor. Her figure was chestnut-colored, outlined in white, all on slightly beige paper. Her sundress was streaked with magenta and yellow, making the green-hazel of her eyes pop. Without any heavy strokes, her features looked like they were floating. Their initials and the date they'd met were written in messy script at the bottom. She thought he'd painted her slimmer in the picture. There was also a mixed CD of Barrington Levy and Tarrus Riley tracks with a few '90s R&B jams thrown in—she loved the Ashanti and Big Pun jam.

So many sweet-sounding tracks that made her run back the nights in his car and decide she would've done it different. Sometimes she wished she'd let it happen in the backseat, just in case he left for school before she could see him again. She talked to Candace, who said she'd been right to say no. Tayla tried to explain how Rolls made her feel.

"You'll feel that way again," Candace told her. Tayla wasn't sure. "You only get one first time and it shouldn't be with a hood rat in the back of a hoopty."

"Don't be bougie," Tayla said.

"You don't be stupid. Lust comes and goes."

Tayla was quiet. They didn't talk about much else. They had never been open about sex in her family.

While grounded and bored, she started to touch herself for the first time. His face would come up out of the darkness of her imagination. His body was absent. She sat and focused on the gentle feeling, humming and warming and building in pulses through her body. She concentrated on the waves as if she could lose them if she didn't. They became more intense, she pressed her fingers harder, small circles trying to coax Rakim's face out of the darkness, and then her bladder felt full and she stopped, afraid to wet her sheets. She wanted to visit him at school and be introduced to his artist friends. She made up her mind to sneak out.

ROLLS DIDN'T SAY shit to his boys, except that, no, he hadn't smashed. They all wondered why she didn't come around any-more and he played it off like it was nothing. He didn't tell them about the texts, that he used smiley faces in the messages, that for some reason they'd gotten carried away talking in the car in-stead of fucking.

Despite her age, he could see her at school with him, holding her own. He lied to his boys, said he needed some new, and they nodded and understood. They told him he better hit that before he left for school again—you know what's gonna happen when you're gone, right? Junior year? They're gonna turn her ass out. He knew that wouldn't happen, not to her, but he sat with the words for a while anyway. He'd been sitting with their words since grade school. It wasn't his boys' fault. He was weak enough to believe them. That was the problem.

His dad asked what the hell had happened to the car.

Rolls said he'd parked it at King's Roast Beef with the cramped lot, and the dent was there when he came out.

The handle?

Rolls was silent.

His next payday was short. There was no further conversation.

He spent his days filling page after page with sketches of Tayla in different outfits—dresses, surgeon's scrubs, judge's robes, butt-naked with stripper heels, construction getups. His favorite was one of her flying a biplane with goggles and the aviator helmet you see in old movies. The curly spirals of her hair billowed from the edges of the helmet, and along the side of the plane, one word, *Freedom*.

Then, on a Saturday in late August, she called and said to pick her up at the Boys and Girls Club.

HE THOUGHT OF bringing flowers, but thought better. He was going to take her to Taco Bell, but as Tayla walked to the car, her red sundress made her look like she was levitating, and people didn't levitate at Taco Bell. They went to Luke's for four-dollar cheeseburgers instead. Not that people levitated at Luke's, but at least they brought you menus when you sat down.

Once they were at the table, the conversation was easy. They talked about Tayla's parents and things at the camera store. Rolls told her he had to photograph a wedding with his dad later that day. He told her he was also getting into graphic design. They had a lot of free refills. Tayla seemed at ease. Whether the date was revenge on her father or not, he didn't really care.

In the car, she kissed him, and the fat softness of her lips pumped him up.

"Let's go somewhere," she said.

"What, like the park?"

"Aww, that's cute," she said. She lowered her eyes.

"It's the middle of the day. There's nowhere to go."

"Your loss," she said. She put on her seat belt and Rolls backed out. Once he was on Exchange Street, he called Dub. Dub was home, but so were his mom, his little brother, and Gio. Rolls looked over at Tayla and said they could use Dub's basement.

She shrank into herself and was silent during the ride. Rolls glanced over a few times to see her chewing her hair. His eyes slid down to where the tops of her tits popped out of her sundress and below to where the looser fabric hid the folds of her stomach. Her brown-green eyes caught the summer sun and brightened. As they reached Division, she started to pick her nails. By the time they got near the Manor, he had to lean over to kiss her on the cheek. "It'll be fun," he said.

THE BASEMENT WAS unfinished. The concrete was painted gray, with flakes and dirt and cobwebs everywhere. She thought the tight space made Rolls seem huge. There were some items stashed in the corners—broken bikes, old lawn mowers, a wheelbarrow with only one handle, some children's toys from the lives of previous tenants, things forgotten.

She touched his stomach lightly. "Here?" she said.

He took in the place and watched her eyes dance around. Her sundress looked diminished.

"Dirt is sexy," he said. "You won't even notice."

"This place is nasty," she said.

She rose to her tiptoes when he grabbed her ass.

"Please," he said. "I'll get a blanket." He kissed the tip of her nose. "I'll be right back."

Before she could nod, he was gone, leaping up the stairs. She told herself it could be worse. It was the person, not the place. Plus, she knew girls who'd lost it on the third-floor steps at school, near where the old athletic equipment was kept. A boy had gotten her up there once. She'd seen the rows of half-sucked Jolly Ranchers on the ledge and left before anything happened.

She turned back to the cobweb-covered windows, so small. It was bright and warm outside, but the cramped, narrow windows made it look like the room was shutting its eyes.

Rolls came back and laid the quilt in the only spot it would fit. A support beam split the space. The blanket was soft—red and white. He leaned her down and knelt between her legs. He didn't take her dress off, just flipped it up. He pulled his pants down until they hung in a bunch at his ankles. His feet reached off the edge of the blanket and he kept his shoes on. The belt buckle sounded sharp against the concrete floor. His hands were patient, though—the back of his hand, his fingernails running along the insides of her thighs, over her underwear. He was focused like he was sitting over a sketch. She thought his movements felt practiced.

The lightest touch shifted her attention down, all the energy in her body moving to a single spot. She waited to feel the pressure of something harder, waited so long that wait turned into want. When the pressure came from the tip of his middle finger, she stopped watching him and tilted her head back.

Rolls loved how her hair fell, how her eyes fluttered. He kissed her stomach and peeled her panties off.

The stairs creaked and she twisted her head to see. "Rakim," she whispered.

He woke out of the dream. She was pointing.

Dub and Gio stood in a small spot of sunlight near the stairs, their bodies so big they made Rolls look small. She flipped her dress down to cover herself. The sun cut across his friends' faces. They both leaned back with their hands on their dicks. Their eyes were locked in.

Rolls sat on his heels and stared down his boys. "The fuck?" he said. He wanted his words back. Wanted something more protective, harsher.

She thought there was some laugh in his voice. For a minute she didn't read it as weakness. She thought he was in on it.

Dub pretended to cover his eyes. G got with it and mocked looking away too.

"I'm not playing!" Rolls said.

His boys didn't move. He knew they'd keep pushing unless he took Tayla and left. She was sitting up, eyes moving back and forth between them. He tried to see his life five years in the future, drive space between him and Tayla, throw her into distant memory, the way most flings pass through our lives. His eyes fixed on her thighs, browner than the last time he'd seen her.

Dub strode over and G lumbered behind him, too big for the space.

"You need help?" Dub said. He smiled like he was reading his paycheck.

Before Tayla could get up, Rolls was rubbing her shoulders.

"No," she said. It came out like a word learned from sex ed. She said it again.

His hands were warm this time, on her face and neck.

"It's okay," Rolls said. "Relax."

She wanted to get up and leave but didn't. Her legs felt cold. She picked at the cotton of her folded dress, coarse like bandages.

Rolls peeled the dress up again and kissed the inside of her thighs. The softness confused her. Some of her sister's friends had been with several men at the same time, even bragged about it, though Candace called them sluts behind their backs. His lips were gentle. His cologne had an old scent.

"Oh, shit, party," Gio said.

Dub laughed. She laughed too, nervously. It was someone else's laugh from somewhere else—her mind racing. She focused on Gio's face, light with light eyes. He was pretty, seemed gentle. Then she couldn't believe she was thinking it and wanted to slap herself straight.

She pulled Rolls' head out of her lap. "I just want you," she managed to say.

Dub smiled and cocked his head. "Don't hurt my feelings," he said.

Tayla looked at him, then back to Rolls. She bunched the dress between her fingers to keep them from sweating. It was the color of a cardinal, a shock of red cloth.

Rolls thought about how soon he was leaving for school and

how Tayla's body curved, smooth-skinned. His boys were poison, but girls liked poison. His dad didn't have enough of it.

"You're beautiful," Rolls said. He searched her face, afraid she'd smell out his game. He took his dick out and began to work it slow.

"Rakim," she said again, but her voice was hoarse, muffled by something. She stared at his dick, then his face, disbelieving that this was going down. She grasped at Candace's words for strength, thought of the way she made men fold. She peered through Dub's legs to the stairs, as if someone else would stop this, but she knew that was a lie. She was the only one.

Rolls watched Gio, who still stared at her, but his eyes seemed warm somehow, still, like he had a different fantasy in his mind. For a second they might have seen the same girl, they might have had the same flutter in their stomachs. Rolls wanted someone else to turn back, but the energy fed on itself. Gio knelt down on Tayla's left, Dub on her right.

All this for what? To avoid being called bitch-made?

Dub began unzipping his pants and she turned toward the noise. "It's all about you," he said. He stared Tayla straight in the eye and she felt her body tense. They were all focused on her, but not really her, some imagined girl. Their eyes were buried in her body.

Rolls started sweet-talking her, leaning to the wrong side— "It'll be a wild story, just see how it feels."

Dub grabbed Tayla's hand, wrapped her fingers around him, and started her in motion. His skin felt softer than she'd expected. She stared at Rakim like she could spit on him. He still wouldn't meet her eyes and then she knew why. Still, some part of her believed he was in control, wanted to believe it. Like this was an adventure and he was a person who could take her out into the world. But he was too weak to look at her.

They made a triangle around her, all on their knees, working themselves with their hands, their frames so large she could hardly see around them. Rolls was between her legs, one hand running the length of her bare thigh, the other keeping himself stiff. She crossed her arms over her chest in reflex, panicked, fantasized about kicking Rolls in the stomach and mashing the other two in her hands. There were footsteps on the stairs, slow and loud. She wanted to scream for help but swallowed the sound. Was she really afraid of these boys who told corny jokes and dated high-schoolers? Rolls wasn't sophisticated. He was grimy. She searched back to the day they'd met for signs, but she was stuck in their presence, the three of them, now. The footsteps trailed off outside. She tried to see where the noise was coming from, but the passage was obscured by Dub's hairy leg. She tried to look past it but he was jiggling himself in her face and laughing.

"Just say hello," he said.

She put a hand up to block him out.

"Play nice," he said, like this was normal.

Her lips tightened, but they were all smiling. Rolls turned her head back. She searched for something soft or questioning or remorseful in his face. Something convincing? There was nothing sweet there. She turned away.

But Rolls brushed the hair back from her ear and moved her head so she had to see his eyes again. He leaned over her and brought his lips to hers, felt their softness. Her legs were spread, heels near her ass, like butterfly wings. Then he let some of his weight on her and she lay back down. She flinched away from his kiss, but even his small frame over her was enough to make her feel pinned. He kept his lips on hers until she opened.

A car started outside.

Rakim? she said in his ear. She must've. He pulled his face back for a second, but the other two still knelt on either side of her head. She wanted to wake Rakim up from wherever he was hiding, make him see the situation as she saw it, as it was.

Rolls ran the edge of his left thumb gently along her lips, told her again to relax. She tilted her head toward the toy trucks and plastic basketball hoop. Dub slipped the spaghetti strap of her dress down so her bra was exposed.

Just get up and walk out, she told herself. Some part of her still wanted Rakim to take control. She was mad for that. She'd had nightmare fantasies before. In those, it'd always been a stranger, and she always fought hard. She looked up at Rakim, who smiled, full, not a smirk. He kissed her below her ear, then slid his face down her stomach, his breath warm through her thin dress. He slid his tongue into her and she felt a pang of pleasure.

ROLLS SAID HE was late for work and left. His boys didn't say shit. He opened the car from the passenger's side and thought about what Tayla's dad would do when he found out. Then he knew she'd never talk. She hadn't said anything to him as he left, just looked through him like clear glass. The day was hot and bright and he was going to get away with this.

Even though he was late, Rolls sat in the car a long time with the windows down, feeling the trapped heat leave slow into the world. He thought about going back for her, but got caught on images of G and Dub in there, still working, each pretending he was alone with her. He imagined rushing down the stairs, turning their faces bloody, but the fantasy left and a weight settled in his chest. *Bitches ain't shit*, his mind looped. It didn't work, though. The weight didn't leave.

His sweat seeped into the cloth seat, or her sweat still on him. He remembered the moment her body had stopped pressing and she just lay back. Nobody made eye contact after that. Rolls imagined it was just the two of them, tried to turn her on. He even felt her stomach muscles ease.

When he finally entered her, she shut her eyes tight and winced. The pain made seams of her body. Just focus on me, Rolls had said.

SHE HAD TO get up. She had to fix herself. She had to get home. She had to get up. She had to fix herself. She had to get home. She had to get up. She had to clean herself. She had to go home.

Dub had left without a word when he finished, sighing loud and walking heavy, not slinking away like Rakim. Tayla and Gio sat in the quiet a minute. She had to get up. She admitted she didn't know how to take the city bus and Gio offered her a ride.

The drive was long and silent and she told herself she wouldn't cry. The car was hot. The AC was broken and she opened a window. Even in the leather seats she felt every bump, squeezing her legs shut to stop the aching. The only words she spoke were *left, right, up ahead*. He still looked pretty. Pretty and sleepy like Rakim had looked those nights in the car. She couldn't believe it. She wanted to scream, but her brain felt muddy and dumb.

The yards got bigger and more manicured as 114 slid into

Cumberland. She straightened the waistband of her dress. She had to clean herself. Gio looked at her and looked away quick. She knew she'd never see him again, never see any of them again.

When Gio turned back she caught his eyes. He opened his mouth, but no words came out. He paused, then asked her which road.

"Bear Hill." She had to get home. She was slowly coming back into her own mind. Her eyes watered from the blocks of air that blew through the open window and she felt herself being erased.

TOLL FOR THE PASSENGERS

...hereditary
All of my cousins
Dying of thirst

        —Kendrick Lamar

On the stretch of pavement in front of my boy Dub's house, the RV hit a car and stuck like a beached whale. With cars parked on both sides, the road was too narrow for it to back out or continue moving forward. My cousins Isaac and Z looked into the spring dusk that stretched fingers of light onto the porch, bearing witness to the failed escape. Maybe that's what vexed Isaac. Maybe he wouldn't have pressed the issue if the boys inside had just acted like men and approached us about it, anyone about it. Isaac was only twenty-six, but he'd been a man almost as far back as I could remember. His face turned to stone as the RV tried to flee the block and drive off into the sunset.

Dub stayed put in the faded green plastic chair. We were all on his downstairs neighbor's porch, where we burned Blacks and drank during the day. In return, Dub let his neighbor crash the house parties we threw even though the dude was in his forties.

A few neighborhoods over, on my street, someone would have

come out, exchanged insurance info, and sent them on their way. Here, they were too far north off Main. We sat around, talked shit, and drank cheap whiskey with ice, just waiting for some drama like this.

Isaac had turned in the years since I'd last kicked it with him. He leaned over the railing chewing ice. I watched him boil, same way our uncle Paul used to before my pops would calm his brother down with that fathead smile and Paul would cool out. I knew better than to try to calm Isaac down. He's the biggest-man-in-the-room type character. I waited to see if my pops' blood would come out of Z. But Z drained his drink and watched Isaac, who swirled the ice in his cup and pressed his stomach over the edge of the railing. Isaac put his cup down slow, pulled his pants to his hips, and bounced into the road. Dub and I didn't really know what was going down, but he followed quick off the porch into the soft, sunlit street. Dub was a world-class instigator, could turn peanut butter against jelly. Z followed them out and stopped in front of the RV. The kin on my pops' side were all giants, and Z was one of the biggest. He waved his baseball-mitt hands and stood like a roadblock, big as a house. My steps were slower. Isaac knocked on the side door and the driver finally put the RV in park and got out. One after the other, six boys emptied out. Girls' voices came from the open windows. The boys wore green pinnies. Some had shamrock glasses on. They looked around at the neighborhood, their necks twisting again and again to take it all in. The sun was beautiful at that hour, but it was falling.

AT SOME POINT, the church and the bars must have gotten all mixed up. Saint Patrick probably never brewed green beer, and

Christians most likely shouldn't get smashed during Lent. My cousins didn't keep Lent 'cause they kept only Christ, and I didn't keep Lent 'cause I had lost Him. Since I'd moved out east with my mom after the split, little by little we let the church go. We were a long way from space and mountains, where I was born, where our family had been whole. We were even further from the house of God.

When my cousins had first turned up on my mom's doorstep, a week before, it felt like they'd brought the church with them. They reminded me of when my mom used to make Bisquick pancakes in the shape of Mickey Mouse, with the butter, syrup, and all. Even back then, when we were little, they still ate her out of house and home.

In the time since, we'd all grown the same, so they were monsters too. Z bear-hugged me like he used to and I felt my feet leave the ground, which I'd thought was impossible. When he set me down, Isaac looked at me with his hat broke off, his lips grinning at the corners. Isaac had more tattoos than me, and right before he wrapped me up, all the initials and dates stretched along his forearms. My mom and auntie Gina, their mom, went way back. Gina was the only one of my aunts who kept in touch, the only one of my pops' sisters who liked my mom. Gina had left the hate somewhere back in Georgia, when her and Pops were coming up, and filled the cavern with breath. She stood big as all of us, but filled with air. When she sang, she emptied it all into her voice and loosed it on the church. I'd go back to sermon just to hear her sing.

The last time I heard her voice, at my pops' funeral, she pulled notes from a room of tears. Her boys picked up and sang on too. I sat and cried like a child listening to them belt out

"Amazing Grace." They had fixed my pops' dead face into a smile—just at the corners, like he kept a secret. That was the end of the Campbell men, the men who sat my ass in church and laughed when I called it Mass.

After my pops' funeral, Gina couldn't fill herself up anymore. Both her brothers had been taken by her God inside of two years, and still, she didn't pick the hate back up. She took the reins. Big Momma laid the weight of the family on Gina's head the same way she'd laid it on her boys and it was too late for her to change and stop laying it. Last time I heard, Gina was fresh off heart surgery, but her voice still sounded strong.

Isaac was wild even before Paul and Pops died, but afterward I think he felt the pressure. He fucked around at a juco, down in the California desert, had to repeat a few semesters of school, and ended up graduating the same year as young Z. Together they booked it out of that San Bernardino heat with thirty Mexican girls' numbers, two diplomas, a proud mother, and lives half in motion.

When they came to see me, it was near the end of a long year and I was visiting with my mom before Easter. They were in exodus. They weren't getting good work back west, felt stuck, so they'd packed up to give themselves a shot out east. Gina was splintering under the weight of Big Momma, and Big Daddy had been funeral-quiet for fifty years. Without Paul and Pop's money, my cousins had to make it happen out here before Gina's load got too heavy and she went the way of her brothers.

THEIR EYES WERE fixed on the RV. When I was little, Isaac told me everyone either builds or destroys. When you get your fingers on something good, you hold on tight. He wasn't in the business of taking things apart. I still remembered him, the night before my pops' service, wide-eyed at 2:00 a.m., scrubbing the church sinks with me because Gina said they weren't fit for a memorial. The RV was sleek beige-brown—my color. It shined like it had just come off the lot.

In the warm weather, things began to melt and unravel. Images trapped in blocks, dragged through from my childhood, came apart in the thaw. I wished that RV had wings. I wanted those frozen memories of my cousins to wait there as they were—Z sitting on Isaac when they wrestled, ants all over our feet in the kitchen 'cause we dropped beans and cold cuts and spilled too-sweet tea and never cleaned up, northwestern summer hail stinging our backs as we booked it out of the park after playing ball. No lost boys. But there was just the beached RV, the narrow street, and dirty water from the spring thaw running into drains.

We stood, the three of us, facing the six. Dub stepped up next to us.

"You hit my car," Isaac said.

"It was an accident," the driver started.

"No shit," Isaac said.

The driver paused. "We're headed to Boston for the parade tomorrow, just looking for a gas station."

Isaac remained silent and sized the kid up.

In the warm spring air, I looked down the length of West Ave., watching time sit on the porches with heavy bodies, pushing them into the small yards that swallowed the refuse of our lives.

"The RV is rented," the driver said.

Z and Isaac turned to each other without words.

"I don't give a shit. Look at my fucking car!" Isaac said.

A stranger's black Camry stood on the street, barely nicked.

"C'mon, Isaac," I said. He shot me a look like when we were young.

"It honestly doesn't seem that bad," the driver said.

"You believe this shit?" Isaac asked Z.

Z shook his head all mournful-like. I clocked the strangers' faces. They started to bunch together. One light-skinned with dreads came to stand next to the driver. A group of kids Dub and I recognized from the Manor started walking down the street— Dub nodded to a few and they broke out in grins. The RV boys watched the crowd forming. The block was swelling.

MY COUSINS HAD been staying with my mom for about a week before the accident. We'd wandered Division in sweats and hoods and white Nikes—camouflaged with the bricks and parks. Since I'd landed a solid job bartending back in Ithaca, I hadn't been coming around much. I missed the way the spring wind teased the laundry swinging from tired ropes below Dominican banners that caught the breeze and slowly pulled apart like Tibetan prayer flags.

Since my cousins had arrived, Dub had bounced around introducing them to folks like he was the mayor. He had us kicking it with all his boys, some who weren't welcome in my mom's house. Each night, after we danced on walls outside the Manor with white girls who didn't know they were white, my cousins and I would come home and they would heat up my mom's cooking—pasta with meat gravy, hamburgers, pork chops. They didn't touch the salad. Unlike my boys, they cleaned up after themselves. Isaac even tried to take the trash out one night but got shook when he saw a raccoon, and yelled, "Oh, shit," so loud that my mom crept down the stairs, creaky as a mother-fucker, to look in our eyes and see if we were high. Isaac ushered her back to bed, Mom's spine bent more than I wanted, telling jokes because I think he wanted to protect us all. Back downstairs, he called me a suburb baby 'cause Mom had moved to Rumford, but I called him a punk for being scared of a damn raccoon.

I didn't know what my cousins had done in those lost years, but as the block filled, the mass of faces rose out to claim them.

The frat boys formed an island in the sea—sleeveless jerseys and green sunglasses. They were already wasted but sobering quick.

"You want our insurance, then?" the driver said.

"I don't trust your insurance," Isaac said.

He took a step toward the kid. At the end of the street, the last rays of sun caught pieces of tombstones in Mineral Spring Cemetery, sparkling off the granite. The kid didn't back up. Isaac's face was reflected in his sunglasses. I inched closer to my cousin.

"How bad you think the damage is?" Isaac asked.

The driver turned his head toward the car. "I don't see any damage," he said.

Isaac walked to the car and squatted down to run his hand over a small dent. He paused. "It's bad," he said.

Before anyone could speak, he stood up and turned fast for the RV. Z pushed aside the driver and was through the group to the door, just behind Isaac. They boarded the RV one after the other. The girls remained fixed in the back. Z filled up the entire walkway.

The frat boys, in their shades and jerseys, piled in behind Gina's boys. "What the fuck!" one of them said. "This is trespassing," another kid said.

Z spun around fast and I thought he was going to swing, but he just stared the kid down until he dropped his eyes.

The dudes from the Manor gathered around the door and in front, blocking them in.

"Relax!" Isaac said to them.

They all started to panic. Isaac stood closest to the girls in back. They looked my cousins over, then locked their eyes on the boys behind, and we all froze a bit, the nine of us packed in with me all the way in the front.

The driver squeezed around Z to reach Isaac. "Can we please go outside?" he said. "Let's talk outside." He was trying to be calm. His voice was low and I could hardly hear him.

"Listen to him, Isaac," I said from behind the group.

"I'm just saying hi," Isaac said, and sat down next to the girls.

There were four of them, all wearing lacrosse jerseys and leggings. They were pretty, or at least three were. The fourth one could've used some sunglasses. Her face was cramped like God had pinched the dough too tight.

Isaac turned to the girls and smiled. "Where y'all headed?"

"I told you—" the driver started.

Isaac paused and pulled that *Try me* look, the one where he clenched his jaw, and his face became lean; then leaned back toward the girls. "Where you coming from?"

Z clocked the small crowd behind him in the RV, arms loose at his sides. They stared past him to the girls.

"What's going on?" one of the girls said.

"You remind me of Jersey girls," Isaac said.

One scoffed.

"You mean trashy?" another said.

"I like Jersey girls," Isaac said. "They don't take any shit."

The scoff girl even smiled a bit. Z still stood facing the crowd and no one else tried squeezing through. My cousin was built like two bouncers.

"You guys don't have enough makeup on to be from Jersey, though," Isaac said.

"All right, what do you want?" the driver asked. He edged closer to Z, trying to get to the girls.

"Calm down, Kevin," Scoff Girl said.

Isaac looked her over and I prayed he'd abandon it all. He smiled. I waited for him to ask her name. I pressed into the frat boys until I was next to Z. Then Isaac slapped his hands on his thighs and stood up, surveying the RV, all the alcohol-red faces and dark shades. He sighed and tilted his head toward the ceiling. He pulled his hat off for a minute and massaged his forehead, then pulled his cap down low across his brow and broke it off to the side again like he was deep in thought.

"Body work is expensive," he said.

"What?" the driver said.

"Compensation," he said. "Two stacks." He looked over the driver at me. "G, tell—"

"They know what it means," I cut him off, then tried to make a joke. "These damn kids and their internet," I said and shook my head like Cosby would've.

Isaac stared at me for a while like he wanted to laugh at my corniness. I wished he would have, wished I were funnier. His real smile was beautiful and soft and would've broke the moment into a thousand pieces.

The driver glanced at his friends.

Isaac finally turned back to the boys and said—"My car's gotta get fixed."

Dub pushed through the whispering boys to stand next to Z and me. With so many people in the RV, nobody could move without hitting somebody else. One of the frat boys turned a light on inside. Night had fallen—the RV still surrounded.

WHEN WE WERE teenagers, I felt like Z would've stopped him. He would have balanced Isaac out before he laid into those boys. Isaac didn't have more spirit than Z, but Isaac had always been volatile. Still, when we were young, Z would challenge Isaac because they were brothers and because Isaac needed it when he got all worked up inside.

A day before my pops' funeral, Isaac was cussing out the owner of the megachurch for leaving the place trashed, but really because his momma was sad her brother would be eulogized in a place so dirty, or maybe just because my pops was gone and they were close. At some point during the yelling, Z wrapped his brother up before the cussing could turn to swinging, and the rawness inside of Isaac melted away.

Z was more like me. He cooked and sang a lot. He and Gina would be two mountains in the kitchen by the stove, pouring the molasses and cutting the ham hocks into the pan of beans, humming hymns together with gentle voices.

Isaac would sit at the table behind a bowl of some sweet cereal and watch. That was years before he began to mark memories on his neck and forearms alongside Bible verses he had known since birth and before. I'd always thought he was made in the image of his namesake—"laugh" in Hebrew, the one waited for, the official son. But a lot had changed since we were kids. Now, that rented laughter had expired and the energy inside him had changed. It had even changed since the funeral. Or maybe it had been changing always and I never noticed.

Back on that cool northwest night when I must've been about eleven, under the stars and sirens, with Isaac's face knotted from his father's blows, he rested in Gina's soft arms while she hummed something so sad that I wondered if we'd feel it forever. That's my memory, his body slung against the rotten wood stairs, draped in his mother's arms, clear-eyed and harmonizing with her voice. I wondered then if whatever had happened to Uncle Bull that made him try and beat the life out of Isaac would happen to us. I wondered if the water that strengthened our roots would dry up, and we'd be like Big Daddy, crossing the country searching for whatever work, only to find that we'd lost Sundays and home. I wanted to remember my cousins as they were before, when they were smaller and the world was smaller and hadn't yet reached through to crack their armor.

Dreads came forward next, took off his sunglasses to show sunken, red-rimmed eyes. His blond-brown dreads looked well kept. Even in the dim yellow glow of the RV, I could tell his eyes were light enough to change in the sun. Our complexion always needs the sun—it eliminates questions. My stomach sank.

"Two thousand is a lot," he said. He stressed the words like he had come to terms with the King's English.

Isaac grinned and Dub smirked, getting excited.

"Not for you," Isaac said.

The kid clenched his fists, flexing his long arms all the way up to his shoulders. He was younger than Isaac—forty pounds lighter too.

"We don't have it," Dreads said.

"You got it." Isaac paused. "Show me your wallet."

Dreads froze.

"That's what I thought," Isaac said.

"Somebody call the cops," the driver said.

Dreads looked at the driver like he'd just yelled "Bomb!" on an airplane.

"Where they at?" Isaac asked.

Dub laughed and the kids from the Manor who'd crept to the door of the RV laughed too.

"Look around you, son," one said. They laughed more.

To his credit, the driver did look around. He shifted his weight a few times, feeling how many layers of people stood trapped behind him.

The RV grew silent and the sound of more voices from the street rose. Cars honked and people yelled and laughed.

"We might have a couple hundred," Dreads said.

Isaac was silent for a while. I got nervous staring at him. He widened his stance. Dreads glanced at me, but I looked away. I knew he'd appeal to me. I got closer to my cousins to avoid it. People shouted from outside, asking what was happening, trying to get in.

Dub yelled—"This is pay-per-view, nigga."

Dreads stared Isaac down and tilted his chin up. With no words he crossed the space to swing, but Isaac had quicker hands. The contact happened in an instant. Dreads stumbled back into his friends. They held him up. The driver reached for Isaac, who leaned away. Before the driver could swing too, Z had put him in a body lock. "Bad move," he said.

Dreads got to his feet to square up again but faltered and almost fell down. He had heart, but he was giving up near fifty pounds to Isaac. People pushed and shoved. I grabbed Dub 'cause I saw him cock his fist back. Dreads' friends held him under his arms to keep him from slumping.

Isaac stood with one fist clenched and drew one hand behind his back. "You ain't want it," he said, lifting his shirt slow. "Don't be dumb."

The people from outside were now trying to force their way onto the RV. "He hit him with the one shot," someone said.

The girls reached for their phones and Isaac turned to them. "Don't," he threatened. "You're cute, not stupid. Don't be stupid." His voice had no shake in it.

I let Dub go and we looked around waiting for someone to leap. The air inside the RV was wet with beer and sweat, and the spring night couldn't press its way to us. We were caged in.

IN THE BED of Uncle Bull's pickup, heading back from cleaning office buildings on a cold night, I sat under the tarp next to Z, where the heat came from. Pops was alive and fat in the front and Bull was okay. In those moments, I was black, or maybe it didn't matter because we were all black and I was my pops' son. Or maybe it didn't matter because we were together and headed to Crack in the Box, all hungry. Or maybe we had just gone and were all full. It didn't matter 'cause Isaac was cracking jokes while our laughter drowned in the jackhammer rumble of the wind against the tarp and our closeness kept us warm.

Now my cousins were scrambling for scraps. Maybe they just didn't know how to ease themselves into a world that kept denting their pride. Dreads and I might've shared some shallow college stories about waking up one morning dehydrated with some dumb shit drawn on our faces, when we stole our friends' Pedialyte and knocked back out, but I didn't know what stories my cousins had. Too much had passed. We couldn't pick up where we'd left things.

"How much do you have?" I asked Dreads.

Isaac was startled out of his focus. The RV stared at me. The frat boys talked. I avoided looking at my cousins.

"We have to count," the driver said.

"I know you got two," Dub said.

"Two." Isaac nodded and stared at me for a minute, daring me to interrupt again. I wanted the block to push off my family, and these boys to leave my city, and my cousins to find space somewhere and something cool and sweet to drink.

The RV boys turned in toward one another and took out their wallets slow. I saw some kids try to leave money in there. I checked Isaac to see if he noticed. Some kids pulled it all out, even the crumpled singles. Isaac and Z were talking low and I couldn't make out what they were saying. I snatched the stack from the driver. Isaac reached to grab it from me, but I turned my back to him and counted it out. The scent of money pulled Dub up close to me. I could smell his hair grease as I straightened the bills. My fingers were cold.

"A little over nine hundred," I said.

"Not good enough," Isaac said.

He reached for his belt again and the driver broke out to hit him. This time Z grabbed him in a choke hold. Everyone watched as he squeezed. The kids tried to pry him off and he started swinging his elbows. I caught the glow from the porch lights along the street outside the RV. I had my phone in my hands. I pressed nine, then one. I looked at my cousins—Isaac ready to swing if anyone touched his brother—then put my phone away. Dub stared me down like he'd seen. It was my mom in me that pressed the numbers to begin with, that's what I told myself. I wanted to stand next to my cousins.

I threw my arms around Z's neck. "Z, stop!" I said.

He let go and the driver fell into his friends, who sat him in a seat next to the kitchenette table. For a moment the group pushed and shoved some more, dangerous close to a brawl. But the next moment they realized, again, what that'd mean. One of the kids shook the driver's arms to help the blood flow back to his head. He must've been a wrestler.

"We don't have any more," the driver said real weak.

I knew they did but said nothing.

Isaac turned to the girls. "You too," he said.

"What?" Scoff Girl said.

"Take out your money," Isaac said.

They weren't shocked and reached for their purses and wallets. One mumbled under her breath and the others were too shook to speak. I came up next to Isaac and held the money out. He watched the four girls fidget for a long time. As Scoff Girl handed him the money, she stared him straight in the eye like he was clear glass.

Z watched Dreads' blood drip onto his shirt from his busted lip. In the dim light of the RV, I could see the gash in Isaac's knuckle pool red and snake down his fingers. Dreads said something through his swelling mouth. I heard only gentle waves, or water, or maybe it was just the hum of the city turning on lights in the night—currents of electricity burning to get away. The narrow street glowed orange. I held the money out to Isaac once more, but he acted like he didn't see, stayed still. Scoff Girl pulled out her phone on the sly and he slapped it out of her hand. She stopped talking. The frat boys slunk into themselves. Z's stone face had broken at last. He looked tired and sad. The money clammed a little in my hands.

Finally I stepped toward Isaac. "Cuz, you took this shit far enough," I whispered.

Our eyes locked for a minute. He smiled, but with something sinister to it. Not the way he smiled when we used to sneak into the fridge and eat pinches of coleslaw on Saturday nights before the church cookout.

"Money's money" was all he offered.

I wanted to rip the bills and scatter them around the RV. Instead, I held the wad at shoulder height and dropped it. The bills started to fall to the ground. Some caught the air and wobbled.

"You crazy?" Dub said like the money was his.

When they reached the floor, Isaac stooped suddenly, began scooping up the bills in a frenzy, making sure none got lost behind feet or in the dimness. Just as quick, he stood up, straightening himself again. He patted his hand on my face. "You're lucky you family," he said.

I stood between the kids and my cousins. Dreads' mouth was swelling awful. His eyes averted. I went to speak but froze. The drama washed over. I started pushing my way through the RV. Z reached out to grab me, but I was gone. Outside, I made my way through the Manor crowd. More people had gathered. They asked me questions, but I ignored them.

The night was gentle. I walked Lorraine until it met Mineral Spring and kept walking. Under the streetlights, a boy with soft hair and brown skin pushed a plastic car down one of the cracked driveways. I wondered who his parents were. What world of stories they spun around him. Maybe his aunt told him, like mine told me, One drop makes you colored, child, and don't forget it. He wasn't old enough to disbelieve it. He wasn't old enough to believe it wasn't about that or be convinced that it was. He probably just laughed and smiled while his aunt dragged her long red nails through his mane, turning his hair into braids. But that was my aunt, and my hair was too fine to hold the braid for long. Maybe he had never heard those words. Maybe he wouldn't need them. The breeze blew and I felt the cool air coming with stories mixed up in it. It was earlier back west and I hoped that Gina was singing—

> *Hop in that water*
> *and pray that it works.*

KINFOLK

By the third penthouse, Dub finally cracked. He turned to an elevator filled with mostly Upper Manhattanites and said, "Y'all live like some fucking rappers."

A few people in the elevator let some laughs go. Dub didn't know that these folks didn't talk about money. Money was all we talked about.

He kept going. "Damn, your parents must be richer than God." He ran his hand along all the elevator buttons and circled the PH.

"Calm down, Dub," I said. I flashed a smile at the two pretty women who were dressed out of catalogs—tight black pants and baggy shirts—smiles perfect like their dentists were family friends. They pretended to be on their phones, or they were on their phones and we weren't even on their radar.

We'd been to two parties already, one of which had a few of those huge Belvedere bottles that look like molten-silver missiles, accompanied by a few plates of capers and lox just for the hell of it. Rolls and Dub weren't about the fish, so we dug in the fridge. Among the mausoleum of takeout containers, we found some fancy cold cuts and cheese and ate them by the fistful. This was the first time I'd invited my boys from home to visit Manhattan with me. We were crashing at Blake's place in Midtown. He was my boy from college and had been showing us around.

When the elevator stopped at the third spot, the door opened right into the apartment. A menacing painting hung above a lacquered wood dresser. Everyone else started to push toward the music, but Rolls stopped for a second to look at the art. It had menace 'cause the blue and purple hues that were layered into the human figure made it look sickly. The figure was swollen and decaying, the skeleton exposed in places. The backdrop was black-green, like the very air in the frame was poisonous. Dub took one look at it and asked how much it was worth.

"It's an Albright," Rolls said, and I smiled 'cause my nigga Rolls could talk artistic circles around anyone.

"So how much it cost?" Dub asked again.

The party had moved on and Blake shot me a look.

"I don't know," Rolls said. "It belongs in a museum."

Upstairs, after a few drinks and a piss, I used my phone to check my bank account, as I had almost every hour since I'd deposited the check the week before. Pops' life insurance came to me almost a year late, but the check sent my mom into tears all over again—twenty-eight grand and change, the fattest check I'd ever seen with my name on it. After the tears stopped, Mom got right back on her grind looking for a settlement from the NFL, but Whit, my little sister from my pops' other woman, and I were still in shock. Whit was getting a lot more. She was set to get paid, and I mean *paid*, at least in our sense of the word, until she hit twenty-five.

As for me, the week before I went to New York, I used fifteen grand to pay back funeral costs, because dying is expensive, then five for unpaid taxes, and I threw the rest in my bank account, which brought the total to $8,732—a nice chunk that could buy a decent car, or a lot of rent, or a damn good down payment on a food truck. That's what Rolls wanted for me. He always said, *You're a food artist, man, embrace that shit.* But he was usually just high and glad that it was my ass doing the cooking for everyone.

Mom hadn't sued Pops' estate for alimony or unpaid child support because that wasn't her style, but she did stay up late into the nights looking through his medical records frantically, the way meth-heads collect rocks and random shit like that when they're out of this world, seeing if she could file suit against the NFL for personal injury or some other negligence. I didn't know if it was about the money or some idea of misplaced justice, but night after night she sat with the documents stacked on the kitchen table and riddled her notepad with doodles of stars and arrows and the 49ers logo over and over. I think she was even upset that my sister was getting paid so much more than me.

I kept waiting to see if the NFL was somehow going to snatch the money back. My mom always talked about the league with bile in her speech. She said the owners wouldn't hesitate to club baby seals to get their money. I tried to tell her that Pops had been a grown-ass man, not a baby seal, really an overgrown-ass man if we wanted to be technical about it.

In the bathroom, I rinsed my mouth out with cold water and took a sip. The countertop was black marble, and my eight grand was still there, shining in bold digits on my phone screen.

On the terrace, Blake handed me a drink. "Cup up, nigga," he said.

I took a sip. "Is this straight?"

"Nah, there's ice."

"Clown," I said, and took another sip. Trap music poured out from somewhere and I tried to figure out if I was looking toward Jersey or Queens. Every elevator ride was like a fucking Tilt-a-Whirl to me—add some liquor, and east, west, north, and south became a real problem.

"Don't babysit." Blake nodded at the drink and I downed it.

"Is that Jersey?" I pointed off out into some skyscrapers.

He laughed for a while. "It's Midtown, nigga."

The only thing I knew about Midtown was that it was hard to catch a cab there and that the Hollands, Blake's folks, owned a palace there—American royalty without the title. Blake was a III, Duke Blake the III of Midtown. That sounded pretty decent to me.

The last time I'd stayed with him, right before his first paralegal contract, we came in during the early-morning hours and I lingered in the hallway, outside the light from the kitchen and the glass living-room walls that looked out over Midtown skyscrapers. I studied a framed quilt for a while. Its borders were worn and it sagged from long use. The frame was made from a dark, oiled wood. Josephine Baker hung across the way in gold and toffee brushstrokes, a soft blackbird with yellow and silver wrapped around her chest and thighs. The poster looked like a marquee advertisement and was in French. I gave up trying to read it. The light rose up gray, bristling underneath the heavy blinds that covered the glass walls, turning the wide windows to eyelids trying hard to stay shut. When I finally made my way into the sitting room, the Hollands' faces were deep in shadow. I heard them swirl their drinks. Blake's pops was up at all hours causing mayhem, enjoying the company of his wild children and the life he'd built. It was four thirty and he had a red plastic cup of liquor. He crossed his legs, then stretched them out and recrossed them in that classy way, with a heel resting on top of his knee.

"I can't do that," I said, nodding toward Mr. Holland's pretzeled self.

He smiled and put a hand through his white hair the same way Blake did. "The key is having no muscle to work against," he said.

We reveled in our drinks and the minutes of predawn, before the sun would chase the calm away completely.

"Have you heard anything about the offer?" his father asked.

"Soon," Blake said.

Mr. Holland took a long sip from his plastic cup, making the ice an avalanche in the quiet. "Just make sure you show it to me." He said it like a king would.

Ballplayers in this country are royalty too—I was $8,732 royal. My pops had never given me the real like that, but I had a few of his old jerseys hanging in my room like regalia. Even though they reached my knees when I was little, I used to wear them to school on show-and-tell days.

Rolls had situated himself nicely into a blunt rotation. When I came up on the circle, the women were already asking him about his artwork. He said if they ever were near Boston, they should check out one of his shows. Then he hit the blunt and talked about how he could be Jain if weed counted as an acceptable vegetable. One of the girls told him that Jains practice abstinence. He leaned in and told her that he practiced Kama Sutra. I told him to stop lying—"The only yoga you know is the dude who sells bootleg DVDs on Central."

Dub came out of nowhere dragging a banker-looking type in a pink polo. "Listen to this," Dub said.

"What?" I said.

"He thinks Pac is going to knock out Money Mayweather."

"Pacquiao throws more punches," Pink Polo said.

"So?" Dub looked at him sideways. "None of those punches are going to land. That slant-eyed motherfucker can't see shit."

The Manhattanites held their collective breath. My chances of getting pussy diminished swiftly. The girls from the elevator were paying attention now. One with dark eyes dropped her jaw in disbelief. I looked to Rolls for help, but he loved it when Dub got going. Like the fake Buddhist he was, he always said the world needed pushing and pulling energy.

"When's the last time you heard of a Chink boxing champ?" Dub kept pushing.

"Not cool, dude," Pink Polo said.

The group glanced back and forth between Dub and Polo.

"Pacquiao is Filipino," I tried.

"Same shit," Dub said.

A blond girl asked if anyone had a lighter. No one answered. I felt people staring at me. Blake was all the way across the patio, surrounded by some kids we'd gone to college with. He was lounged back smoking a cigarette like the motherfucker could not be more comfortable. I turned to Rolls. He took a sip of his drink and grinned.

"Plus, it's better business if Pacquiao wins," Polo finally said.

"We talking about boxing, not business," Dub said.

"Sports are business. Don't be naive," Polo said.

Dub sucked his teeth. "Man, you don't know boxing," he said. He was quiet a minute like he'd been made a fool. "It'd be like

G over there, all skinny and slow and feeble, freshman-ass brain, trying to go rounds with me," he said.

I put my hands up and before any of the Manhattanites knew what the hell was happening, we were slap-boxing like back in high school. In a real fight, all bets would've been off, but Dub lunged too much and dropped his hands when he slap-boxed. Plus, my arms were a lot longer and I'd boxed for real when we were growing up. He was shorter, stockier, the football-build type. People backed away and gave us space on the deck. True to form, Dub kept lunging and I kept leaning back and hitting him with counters.

"You guys do this for fun?" someone asked.

Rolls said yeah. I started to hop in my step, just bounce a little, and it must've pissed Dub off 'cause he tagged me with a closed fist. I lost my balance a bit.

"How that feel?" he said.

I got back in my stance and hit him with a right so hard, the slap rang out loud.

"Don't get knocked out slap-boxing!" Rolls said.

Dub always bragged that he'd never lost a fight. He lowered his shoulder and speared me backward. I felt his low center of gravity lift me off my feet for a second. My lower back hit the railing. I grabbed hold of him to try and weigh myself down.

"Easy. Dub. Homie. Nigga. Easy!" I yelled.

Rolls had come over quick and grabbed my shoulder. Dub relaxed and I eased back onto my feet. My tailbone felt warm—a bruise was forming. Most of the party had taken notice and were staring at the three of us huddled near the railing. My hands felt slick on the metal.

"Damn, you sounded like a bitch," Dub said.

Blake approached us.

"Why you gotta do that here?" he said. He looked us over while I turned to peer over the side of the railing.

I couldn't even see the street below, it was so high, just the lights, blurry and distant. I squatted with my hands above my head, gripping the guardrail. I kept breathing until my heart slowed down. I tried to survey the party, and the tight-dressed girls had already forgotten us.

Blake put a hand on my shoulder. "Let's get you high," he said.

COCAINE IS A drug that never gets saved. When someone has white around a bunch of people who do it, faces start popping out of closets and windows like a Disney musical. Rolls didn't partake—no one did where we were from—but against all odds, Dub tried it and, like all human beings, loved it. So despite Rolls trying to talk me down from buying more, Blake and Dub had me walking to the ATM just after midnight. Four hundred of my pops' death-dollars later, we were at another apartment surrounded by Duke sorority girls Blake knew.

Rolls sat down on one of those black leather boxy couches that are better to look at than sit on. He flipped through a *Vanity Fair*. The rest of us sat around the kitchen table, and Blake clapped me on the shoulder. "Break it out, break it out," he said.

When I broke out the three bags, Rebecca, a girl Blake had introduced me to not five minutes back, put a soft hand around the base of my neck like I had whipped out an engagement ring. Her lips were covered in crimson. Against her milk-pale skin, the color made her look like a sexy vampire. Her hair smelled like lavender when she leaned close.

Their bathroom was smaller. These girls were living on their parents' dime, but not in their parents' homes. All the blood vessels in me had tightened, making the closed space feel even smaller. I drank handfuls of water, splashed it on my face and neck. The money was still there, most of it. Including the gas and food I'd bought, it was down to $7,989.

I thought about my pops' old game stats. I used to look at them on the back of his playing cards and imagine what it cost his body. I read that he had an eight-sack season and I saw the hobbled stride he walked with on the rare occasions when I got up with him. Five pass-blocks left me with the image of the way his left arm drooped—a rotator-cuff tear that he played through. Back then the surgeries weren't arthroscopic yet. His body was riddled with scars thick as butter knives. I figure my mom pictured those scars every time she went through his medical records. She knew the doctors by name—the good, the bad, the un-Hippocratic. She begged him to stop playing before he was ground down to nothing, but he never listened. Sometimes I think it was the celebrity, but it wasn't. He was just a man doing what he was put on this earth to do and loving it. At the end of his life, the scars were nothing more than old decisions forgotten. My mom said it was never even an option for him to quit 'cause he was never about the fans or the money. He was about the game. He knew football and the Gospel. I never got to ask him much about either.

At the table, Dub was talking a mile a minute, running his mouth like my aunts when they got excited in their preaching.

Rolls got up from the couch and pulled me aside before I could sit down. "Yo, let's dip," he said. "Dub's out his mind." His eyes looked red-tinted, a little low. It was just after one.

"Why don't you try some? A little pickup." My voice sounded tight.

"You know I'm not touching that." He looked at me sideways.

I knew he was right. I wanted them to see New York like I did, but I had told myself I wouldn't do white around them.

"That shit's gonna get you in trouble," he said.

"Thanks, Deepak."

"I'm not fucking with it," Rolls said.

"Dub tried it," I said.

"Yeah, and he looks like a fucking lame."

I looked over and almost on cue Dub yelled at me, "G, freestyle for these ladies!"

Rolls raised his eyebrows and pulled his lips in. Dub was the type to get fucked up and tell us his secrets. Those were the only times he was in his feelings. Those were the only times he talked to Rolls and me about his family.

"I told them you the nicest!" he said.

"Please—" Rebecca held out the yay. "Freestyle for us." Her body bent in a way that outlined her slender frame. That was enough for me. Rolls tried to whisper to me and Dub cut him off.

"Stop being soft," he said.

My eyes moved between the two of them. If we were alone, Dub would've added "nigga." He was learning. He looked like he was on an album cover—leaned back in his chair with girls passing a plate of coke around him. I thought about his girl, Simone, but they stayed on that on-and-off-again shit, so I decided not to think the worst. The dish and straw made the rounds. Sniffling sounded. I dragged Rolls over with me.

"Blake, gimme a line and a beat," I said.

Blake started beat-boxing. Dub clapped. Rolls sandwiched

himself between two brunettes and tried to hide a smile. Every-one leaned in as I ad-libbed early on to catch the rhythm.

I rhymed about doing white-girl with white girls, about bring-ing some black boys into a white world. I rhymed about walls decked out like museums and how men from our station rarely see 'em. I rhymed about long nights and long weekends, about playing our roles so that they don't sanction our per diems.

At this point the girls had their phones out recording. The lights clicked on and the mechanical eyes pointed, poised to cap-ture me. The plate of white clanked down to my left. Blake sped the beat up a little bit.

I started kicking dumber party raps. I rhymed about drinking till we forget woes, about getting wild enough to throw blows. I probably rhymed it with more blow, then rhymed it with some-thing stupid, like *fresher than shell toes*. I probably rhymed a cliché about having a dope flow and about how even the pope know.

Then I started talking about Pops. I rhymed how he never heard a single punchline, about how them football lights musta felt brighter than sunshine, or maybe I rhymed about how he ne-glected to give his son time, about how he never heard a stanza, act, not one rhyme.

Someone reached over and pulled the plate away.

I kept rhyming about my family in hearses and curses and what a nigga worth is, if it's all worth it, or if black skin make our legacies worthless.

And then Blake stopped the beat. Rolls was staring at me. Dub looked like he wanted to slap me. The girls had put their phones down and Blake scraped his insurance card on the plate, lining up more white. He took a little and passed the plate.

*　　*　　*

WHEN WE GOT stuffed into cabs to go downtown to Live, Rolls and I ended up in a car with two random Deltas. I tried to get into the cab with Rebecca, but her friend stiff-armed me out the way. Of their group, I voted her friend most likely to go through a white-girl-in-dreadlocks phase. I sat next to the driver, and Rolls tried to talk to me through the thick plastic.

Rolls leaned forward to the gap in the divide. "Why the fuck we going to a club at one?" he said.

"This ain't home." I smiled and bent my head toward the space so he could hear me better. "Little Rakim, you're not in the Bucket anymore."

He didn't laugh or even smile. The cab started taking us down the West Side Highway. The girls didn't try to make conversation. They were on their phones. I'd taken another hundred out before we left and checked my account now—$7,889.

"Be careful with that money, G," Rolls said.

The dark body of river ran outside the window, streaked by the orange glow of the city, the night here always shades lighter.

"G?"

"Yeah."

"For real, don't blow that," he said.

"Miss me with that moral shit."

In the rearview, he twisted the small locks in his hair. The cab got off the highway.

"Don't act like a rich bitch," he said.

"Fuck you."

"This is just one night to them."

I turned back to face him. He was serious. Even in the dim, I could tell he was for real. The tiredness had left his eyes. I felt low from the coke blues.

"I—"

"You're not a wise man," I cut him off. "You're just a nigga who takes pretty pictures."

Now the girls were paying attention to us. The driver even broke his autopilot to smirk, like he'd expected this from us.

Rolls nodded. "Aight," he said. He kept nodding.

After my pops' death, Rolls' pops, Rev, hugged me when I came into his camera shop, right there in front of all the customers. We'd never hugged and I froze a bit. He felt small in my arms, same build as Rolls. That nigga would be skinny for life. In the back of the shop, neither he nor Rolls said sorry, but they let me talk about my pops for a long while. I remember Rev looking at his son intently, maybe thinking about how he'd raised Rakim. Finally, he said that he was going to give the shop to him if he wasn't too busy being an artist. Rolls smiled. I did too. We were still too young to know who we'd become.

AFTER THE CAB I was down to $7,866. We took a few more bumps then talked to the doorman outside of Live. He said the minimum for bottle service was a thousand. Otherwise, a group that large wasn't getting in. The girls waited for us to make a move even though some of them could've paid the price a hundred times over before their parents noticed. But that wasn't protocol for pretty women.

I turned away from the girls toward Blake. "Split it with me?"

Rolls went to speak, then turned back to the girls.

"I'm in law school," Blake said, as if somehow that took his family's money out of the equation. Still, I knew his dad kept tight tabs on him.

Some of the girls approached us. "B, we're going to meet my friend inside," one said.

Blake said aight and turned to me. *We go through too much bullshit*, he sang. *Just to fuck with these drunk and hot girls*. He knew I liked that hook.

Dub talked to the remaining ladies. I sized up the men dressed in the uniform, button-ups tucked into some smooth-looking jeans and blazers. Then I looked at my boys. Rolls was skinny-jeaned down like a weirdo rapper, and Dub had some colorful LRG on. We looked like artists. Too bad we didn't have the kind of artist money you needed to get into a spot like Live. An upbeat mash-up cascaded out the door, and dance lights flashed behind the huge garage-type windows.

Dub approached me all frantic. "They're gonna leave if we don't get a table," he said.

"Leave where?"

"Some shit about friends. I ain't listen," he said.

I cut my eyes at his high ass and thought about going home with Rebecca, thought about getting treated like I had fans, maybe just like I had money.

"You'd still have plenty left," Dub said.

"It's not your money," Rolls said out of nowhere.

"Go readjust your chakras," Dub said.

Rolls started to correct him, then paused.

"Guys, we gotta make a decision," Blake said, as if that nigga was pitching in.

"You're coked out," Rolls said.

"And you been acting like a bitch since we got here," Dub said.

"All right, guy," Rolls said. He fought with words, was a de-escalator.

The girls drifted away from us. I jogged over and tugged Rebecca's dress.

She leaned back. "Oh, hey. What's up?" She glanced at her friends.

I held my phone out. "Let's meet up later." I wondered how my pops had talked up women. It probably wasn't like that. She put her number in my phone. Blake came over to corral the rest of the women and I bounced back to my boys. "You too thirsty," Rolls said.

"What's good?" I said.

Rolls and Dub both looked at me, then at the iceberg of white girls floating back to familiar waters.

The doorman came over. "You guys gotta either buy a table, get in line, or get the fuck out of here," he said.

I recognized the next look that settled into Dub's face. His eyes went dead, like his brain had shut off. He wasn't the de-escalating type. He leaned his weight forward and got big. The bouncer stared him down, lights from inside flashing behind him.

I grabbed Dub quick and we were gone. As I pulled him away, I yelled to Blake, and he turned from the women to catch up with us. Dub wasn't normally that easy to pull away, but he was busy trying to keep coke snot from coming out his nose and mumbling shit about the bouncer being bitch-made. Blake told him it was just how shit worked out here. Even high, Dub's eyes flashed with recognition.

I loosened my grip on Dub and asked Rolls if he wanted to go back to Blake's. He didn't even look at me. But when we passed a food stand that smelled like falafel, he perked up.

"This could be you," Rolls said.

"You're open," I said.

"What?" Rolls said.

"I don't fuck with halal. And, nigga, this is New York, eight grand doesn't even buy a food stand."

Rolls was silent and I wished I'd said something nicer.

After a few blocks, Blake ducked into a dive bar and we followed him. Behind the bar there were pitchers of Long Island iced tea for five bucks a pop. The floor, tiled and slick with mud and water, was packed with underage kids and old-timers who looked like they'd been growing from the bar stools for years. I bought my boys a round of the poison and left the tab open. We found a booth in the corner and squeezed together.

A big-titted woman in a maroon dress slid around on the dance floor with a boy half her age. Nina Simone pumped on the busted speakers. Those people on the floor walked just like them horns played. *Blossom on the tree, you know how I feel…It's a new dawn. It's a new day.* I wandered away toward the bathroom on that voice. I was never much for the baptism my pops' family preached, but I was all about blues and Gospel. Voices that made you believe they were telling the truth and nothing else.

The bathroom was trashed. Garbage everywhere and overflowing the can. Graffiti covered every inch of the walls and covered it again. The toilet lid was ripped off so I stood right there at the sink with my phone out. Instead of checking the account, I began reading the walls. There were so many layers. It was hard to catch full statements. One line read, *Go home, Mom, you're drunk.*

Then I checked my account. The new charges hadn't cleared. The tab was open, but I could've gotten all of Pawtucket drunk in a bar like that. I read more names on the wall until they started to blend together.

The names were splattered so thick it started to look like tie-dye. Dub didn't know his pops' name. His mom refused to tell him. I wanted to leave my pops' name on the wall, maybe just #90, his jersey number. The way most folks remembered him.

My pops was immortalized at his alma mater. The Morris Trophy for Pac-10 defensive player of the year is made of glass. My mom used it as a doorstop for my room. Her house is old and lopsided and the doors don't shut well or stay open. She learned football just to communicate with him. She used to smoke French cigarettes and wear a hijab, more concerned with mountain views and social activism than blitzes up the B-gap.

THE MULTICOLORED CHRISTMAS lights made the bar warm, shut off from the rest of the city. The woman in the maroon dress and the boy were now strutting to some flighty James Brown—"Get On the Good Foot." Dub was animated, talking to Rolls. My boys were laughing. I bought another round, this time for everyone in the place. A few folks lifted their drinks but most went on without notice. I sat back in the booth and we finished the bag. Rolls didn't do any, but he didn't screw his face up either. I was with my boys and there was possibility ahead of us, not behind.

I bought a third round. Rolls was slumped, and Dub told me to chill. He said to think about tomorrow. Blake got up and went to the bathroom.

"An hour ago you were asking me to drop a grand on some bitches who didn't even know your ass," I said to Dub. My speech felt thick and it must've cut deeper than I thought.

Dub's gaze looked far away, like his eyes were fumbling

around the world blindly. I pushed him in the booth, somewhere between playful and hard. His eyes livened a bit.

Rolls woke up from his weed-head slumber. "Let's go get some food," he said.

Blake came back from the bar and handed me my card.

"I signed for you," he said.

"Fuck you too," I yelled. I stood up.

"Sit your soft ass back down." Dub grabbed my arm to pull me back and I shoved him again. He grabbed both my arms so I was trapped in the booth. I yanked my weight back to stand but couldn't because he had leverage. He laughed.

The bartender saw and told us to quit fucking around. I stood up slow, straightened my shirt, and looked down on my table of friends. I wanted to knock Dub's teeth out.

WHEN MOM AND I walked through the Husky Hall of Fame in the days after Pops' funeral, she didn't talk about nursing Pops back to health after rough games. She just kept yelling "U Dub!" like she was back in college, smiling about the positive. She talked about the burger joint, Dick's, that her and Pops used to go to and how they used to sneak tequila into the old Husky stadium by packing it into my pops' roommate's bag—he was in a wheelchair from a diving accident so no one checked him. Mom held my hand as we walked the bleachers like I was a kid again, pointing out to Lake Washington as the spring sun set, turning the lake into a postcard. She pointed out the Cascades to the east. She never talked about his football accolades except to say that she wished I'd seen him play. At the funeral, his hall-of-fame coaches forgot his name. They called him Lane.

* * *

BLAKE AND ROLLS dragged us to some benches near the High Line. Dub hopped around, and I felt low. I texted Rebecca. *What's good?* I wished I'd said something witty. I wished we spoke the same language. Rolls kept saying I needed to throw up and I told him to shut the fuck up. He and Blake sat Dub and me down on different benches. I stared at Dub over my right shoulder and imagined caving his eye in. Blake ignored us and called his old girl a few times. He wanted pussy. We were all too fucked up to be good to our people.

Rolls started pacing behind the benches and mumbling to himself about green space in cities. Everyone tuned him out.

"Get higher," I told him.

"I'm sober," Rolls said.

Dub and I looked at each other.

"You louder than the Fourth of July, nigga," Dub said.

Dub and I almost smiled at each other.

"You're so high, you'd pipe a vending machine," I said.

Dub laughed a little. "Nigga, you blaze so much, your connect thinks you need an intervention."

Blake hung up his phone. "Lauren's on the way," he said. He looked up from his screen. "And you smoke so much, your emergency contact is Domino's, nigga."

"Yeah, yeah," I said. "You smoke so much, niggas think you Cherokee."

"Nah, nah," Blake said. "You hotbox the car so often, the pope gets scared when you open the windows."

Dub didn't laugh. I tried not to—that was the kind of intellectual shit that made me suspect in high school. Dub and I stared at each other again. Blake tried to make some joke or explain it, but the traffic rolled past, hissing like an expensive sleep track.

Then the street sounds eased for a minute and the night fell silent. Dub slumped off the bench, so drunk that he could only be swimming in his mind, nowhere else.

"Your mom traded you for goodwill," I said.

Dub sat up from his slump, glared at me. Rolls shook his head.

"Your mom was a fucking side chick," Dub said. He tried to make a move, but he was stumbling drunk and Blake held him down with both hands.

I thought about my pops' other women and about my sister. I spat at Dub but it didn't reach him on the other bench.

"Cool out," Rolls said.

"Your pops was a bridesmaid," Dub said, and I wanted to push his fish eyes through the back of his skull. Wanted him to lose everything he had. I tried to shake my head clear of liquor. I couldn't.

"Ayo, what's your pops' name again?" I asked, real calm-like.

Rolls stepped away from me. Dub'd only told us what little he knew about his pops when he was dead drunk, back in high school, those nights Rolls and I funded the parties he threw at his house.

Blake studied us, trying to figure out what'd been said.

Dub was silent.

"What was that?" I said, cupping a hand to my ear. "Your pops could kick you in the fucking head and you wouldn't even know. He dropped you off like an order of lo mein."

Dub was tongue-tied. I couldn't remember another time. Rolls just shook his head like his well of wisdom had gone dry. Blake didn't look at me.

I got up and started walking underneath the High Line, headed north. I went to check the account but stopped. Even after the bill for the drinks cleared, that'd be a whole lot of something, or nothing.

There was a lot I'd never know about Pops—what lines he laid on women, how he and my mom came to share something. I let my memories of him run on loop, playing together to re-create him. He took me to see a horror movie when I was twelve. He'd brought a bag of Jack in the Box egg rolls into the theater. Freddy Krueger kept killing bad actors and I watched Pops suck those things down. He caught me watching and offered me the bag. He yelled some shit at the movie screen with his mouth half full and I took a bite of one and we both laughed and stayed laughing. His laugh was a hoarse, full-bodied affair. It was like watching the earth tremor. Yeah, I could hold on to that.

OUTSIDE TACOMA

The world is fully lit and I can still smell the liquor on my stepmom. Dee's eyes are hidden from the summer sun behind some dark-ass shades and her voice is two octaves below tires on gravel, even lower than usual. I laugh to myself 'cause I know when we get to my pops' storage unit, my mom will bitch and lecture her. That's her MO. In the backseat, my sister, Whit, fourteen, is on her cell phone. She doesn't smell a thing, or maybe she's numb to it. I wish I'd woken up early enough to ride with my mom, but even after flying in from RI, she managed to keep farmers' hours and was gone from the La Quinta before I got up.

Dee belts out, *How do you want it, girl,* singing along with the radio. Dee's dress straps slide real awkward on her vanishing frame. In the rearview mirror, Whit rolls her eyes at the performance. She's been surrounded since birth.

Dee whips the rental Mustang around curves like a giddy teenager. Living in Vegas the past year has turnt her up. Her license was reissued only three months ago and already she is enjoying the invincible, morning-after drunk drive.

I ask how her night went, but the station throws on "Let It Burn" and she starts rambling about Usher, little femme this, soft in the lips that, etc. She swerves.

I crack the passenger window and take in the clean Washington morning to keep from staring at the speedometer. The roads are wide and coarse, tires working over the pavement so heavy I can feel the vibration.

Whit joins in and starts talking about another pop star, one I've never heard of. They're throwing comments back and forth and Dee isn't watching the road. Neither of them misses a beat.

I turn to ask Dee to slow down. Before I can, she slides me a cellophane bundle of painkillers, Perc 30s, the ultimate, each one smaller than a pencil eraser, guaranteed to make the entire world your personal couch. They're a good way to lose touch, first with your body, then with your troubles. It's like going limp in the jaws of a bigger animal.

"How'd you get these?" I ask.

"I'm in pain, sweetheart." She looks at me and her glasses are mirrors, too big for her face. She's always had a link on goods that border reckless—chop-shop cars, wholesale ammo, piss-cleaning tonic. She tells me to pop a few.

I don't admit I'm familiar. Plus, a few of these will have you vomiting on your Sunday clothes. When I visited Dee and Whit in the desert last Thanksgiving, they hadn't made the small town house a home yet. It had been a few months since Pops had died and they'd come down to Vegas from Washington, but they were still living out of boxes, no food in the house. When he was alive, Pops had always done the cooking. Dee wore a black-and-white dress and got us tickets to the Cirque show, the one dedicated to the King of Pop. But then she threw up on herself at dinner, and just Whit and I went.

I look at my sister in the rearview and almost give the pills back. But Whit keeps texting without even looking up. The car bumps over the breakdown-lane grooves and I tuck the pills into my pants pocket and wish she had better kin.

LAST YEAR, AFTER my pops' funeral, my mom and Dee made sure his storage was locked down from the rest of the family, afraid it'd be picked clean like carrion. But we avoided sorting it until now. I think Dee and Mom wanted to wait because they thought Whit and I couldn't handle it. Maybe they couldn't handle it themselves. Whit and I shared the feeling that if we pieced together the scraps of Pops' life we might become brother and sister for real, and our cousins and aunts on Pops' side would become family again and we could keep it moving. At least I felt that way—I just imagined it for her.

A man at the funeral, an uncle or cousin, wearing a yellow dress shirt with a teal tie, gathered us together after the service. He told us not to let the gaps form and handed out his number. Then he hugged Whit and me and left the reception. We never talked about it.

After the service, Mom flew back to RI, and I flew back to Ithaca, back to substitute teaching and bartending at the Good Life, to serving watered-down drinks to kids with fake IDs, waiting for something better. At that point, Dee and Whit were still up in Washington, on the edge of the cliff. I picked up my car at Rochester International and drove I-90 away from Lake Ontario thinking up corny-ass metaphors about my people and solitude, passing by secluded towns nestled just off the highway behind groves of trees in the near darkness. So close to the traffic, but out of sight. A few months after the funeral, Dee and Whit moved out to Vegas. Whit and I let the gaps form.

* * *

129

BIG AL, THE storage man, remembered how my pops had won the Rose Bowl for the Huskies in '84. He let the storage slide for a year free of charge, but it got to the point where he laid down ultimatums—ship it, sell it, or sort it. So we all flew back out to Washington to get on with it.

Dee's arm draped on the steering wheel is skin and bones. She lights a cigarette. It's good—slows her down some. Her lipstick marks up the beige paper. Sometimes Mom talks about my pops' other women. It's the only time I hear venom in her voice. But I only know Dee, and that was by the book, after my parents split, so the story goes. No one else ever came around and I never got around to asking him. Then after he died, all of a sudden Mom's memory became real rosy—Pops the bighearted gentle giant. Whit remembers him like that too, I don't know how. But until recently, she's been on the periphery of my life so I can't claim to see what she sees. That one's on me. She's only fourteen. I'm twenty-three.

In the rearview, her eyes stay fixed on her phone. Outside of my aunt's face being etched in hers, I don't know much at all about Whitney. I could lie and say it's the age, but I don't know a damn thing about the scale she uses to weigh the world.

This past spring, a girl at her school climbed one of the light poles at the football field and jumped off. Even though Whit didn't know her well, she stayed home a few days after that. I checked up on her then, but Dee said Whit was doing good. By her final report card, she'd raised her failing grades. Dee always tells her about me—how her brother was an English major at an Ivy League school and how she should send her papers my way. Dee throws dirt on my name too—that I drink too much and spend too much money on women—but she throws dirt on everyone. I'd like to help with Whit, but our correspondence fades in and out.

The day is heating up. When we arrive, the storage unit is packed end to end like a good cannoli.

My mom stands with her hands on her hips, same way my nonna would've, glaring at Dee. "You look awful," she says.

"Shut up, Letty."

But Mom's right. Dee's weave is a little crooked.

"How late were you out?" Mom says.

I think Dee's about to hand me her shades, take off her earrings, square up. "None ya damn business," she says.

Mom looks to me.

"What a great day," I joke.

Whit's eyes are wide, staring at the mess, and she pays no attention. Dee brushes by my mom to look at the unit.

It's too early in the day to pop pills, but I feel them there in my pocket—even just a half could help ease the shit.

Mom fans her hand in front of her nose. "You smell like a bar," she tells Dee.

"Yeah, and you smell like a prude."

I step over and make a mock show of shielding my mom, patting her head. Her hair is thinning, and worrying has kept the weight off. For a minute, I'm nostalgic for the days when my boys would play-flirt with her. I smile at Dee. "Look at you two lovebirds," I say.

"Boy, shut up," she says. "You know damn well I'm not in the mood." She takes the mess in.

My mom has already made a small pile.

"What's that?" Dee asks.

"Just some things I thought Gio might want," Mom says.

Dee bends down and picks up a crystal vase. "Your son wants the Baccarat?"

"I bought that in California," my mom says.

"With Lonnie's money," Dee says.

Whit turns around and draws out an *Oh*, the drama gets her attention.

"Well, maybe if you got here on time," Mom says proper-like and walks into the narrow space she's cleared already.

Dee stares at me, and my face looks round in the lenses of her shades. "Your mom is a greedy bitch," she says and turns back toward the car.

"Hey—" I start but Dee keeps going.

"Fuck this shit," she says. "I don't need this. Waking up at the crack of dawn like you're fucking treasure-hunting. It's just a damned storage unit, Letty. You need to get laid."

I am torn between laughing and defending my mom, who should've reignited her life a while back.

Whit runs to hug Dee, one of those full-body hugs where you fit your whole self into another person. My mom's shoulders slump, so I go over and throw an arm around her. She keeps her eyes on Dee, face tight with poison words swallowed.

Dee says something to Whit that I can't hear, then pushes her off, wobbles, enough so I think she might fall, and opens the car door. She's racing somewhere. It scares me because I know the feeling well. So did my pops, who died in the ring throwing haymakers at the thing. I've been there myself, cracking jokes while sinking into something murky.

Dee starts the car and rolls down the window. She looks at us a second, then turns up the radio and leaves, peeling out of the row—still driving invincible.

Whit begins taking some pictures of the stuffed unit with her phone.

"What a great example she's setting," Mom says. I say nothing and she asks me how late Dee was out. I tell her I don't know. She asks Whit too, then softens and asks me if I think Dee is all right.

"She's a grown-ass woman," I say.

Mom drags out a crushed box from a heap of shit. "If she wasn't going to be here, why'd she even come out? We were supposed to do this together."

I dig into a box of my bloodline. "Yeah, well, now we're not."

July in Washington isn't that hot, but the storage unit is an insulated toaster and Pops saved everything—blank Polaroids, backpacks with broken zippers, old newspaper articles about him, Narcotics Anonymous pamphlets, check stubs from his playing days made out to all sorts of family members I've never heard of, some '80s gear that I snatch and rock without shame, and every piece of mail ever addressed to him. No lie, he saved autograph requests and delinquent phone bills alike. He even had one of my high-school report cards that I don't remember sending him. It's like he'd planned to hit the whole world back—he just waited too long.

The three of us move with ease and quickness. It's efficient. No pageantry. Whit does take a few pictures of us together in Pops' old clothes for her various apps. I strike dumb poses to make her laugh.

Big Al says he'll ship the stuff to us at cost, so we leave him a signed Rose Bowl poster with all the Huskies' signatures. He is a U Dub fan like everyone else in this state. He loved my pops, even gave him and his brother-in-law a job cleaning office buildings after the football money dried up. Maybe he still loves him, in his own way, like we do.

Dee is the type who would've objected to the gift, claimed the poster for herself, made the room hot. She was a social worker for years and maybe it made her tough. Now she's unemployed and has been living off the NFL life-insurance checks since Pops died. I plan to ask Whit about the checks, make sure the money is getting to her, but when I bring Dee up, she gets defensive.

Once I started drinking and carrying on, I grew to like Dee. She keeps a .30 cal. revolver on her at all times, like she's about to break through the swinging doors of a saloon and apprehend an outlaw. I've seen her put all six rounds into the ten ring from twenty yards. I respect her for that. Still, I want to tell Whit I hope she inherits just the right amount of her mother, not a fingernail more. I don't want to wait too long to tell her.

WE GET BACK to the La Quinta late in the afternoon. The day is hot, summer sun still high. There is no sign of Dee. Mom calls her behavior childish but then backs off and tries to finesse the situation. My mom is a schoolteacher and has always been good with kids. She decides my sister and I need some alone time and leaves the hotel to give us space, disappearing into the strip-mall wasteland near the hotel. We crank the AC and watch *High School Musical*.

I talk to Whit about school for a while. She says she hates it, every single fucking subject. She was suspended for throwing a textbook at a racist redneck boy, then for spitting on another one, and again for cussing out a teacher she thought was racist. She lies close to me, her eyes slanted like all the women on my pops' side—face wide and flat with smooth skin. Dee looks different, has those big eyes, full of changes.

Whit says her mom isn't answering her texts, asks me to hit her up. I do, then I put my arm around her and she tucks her chin against my chest.

"What was that girl's name?" I ask.

"What girl?"

"The one that climbed the light." I watch her face for a reaction. I'm thinking about Whit climbing. We all have our edges. Dee and I are two pills away from ours, or two pills safe from it. I kiss the top of Whit's head. I hated her blond highlights, am glad that her weave is black now.

"Hannah." She keeps her eyes on the TV. "I didn't know her well."

"Still." I turn the volume down. "You gotta think about it."

"My mom talks like that sometimes," she says.

"Like what?" I ask.

She picks at her gaudy nails with rhinestones in the polish. "I don't know." She is backing out on me. I keep silent and just let her lie still awhile. "She cries a lot." Whit is too big to really curl up, but she brings her knees in tighter. "Sometimes she says no one will ever love her again," Whit says. She tilts her head to face me and I don't know how to respond.

The pills in my pocket feel like mints in the cellophane wrap. At thirty dollars apiece, I've seen houses get pawned clean for the high. It's the only drug that's ever pushed me to a place where hunger—real, spiritual, or otherwise—doesn't exist, like a pocketful of Tibet.

When I visited Dee and Whit over Thanksgiving, instead of spending time with my sister like I should have, I got faded on Crown Royal with Dee and hit the Strip with some artist types I knew from Cornell. I took the benzos Dee'd given me and lived a second life. I threw up in the sand and drove home. Dee tucked me in on the couch and cranked the heat to eighty like we weren't in the fucking desert.

I rock Whit awkwardly. "Were you scared?" I feel like a shrink. I can't picture Dee crying, can't separate that image from the woman cussing at the storage unit.

"Those lights are really high," she says. "And nobody saw her do it. Some kids just found the body."

Neither of us saw our father die. Whit got the news by phone. Mom showed up on campus after one of my Black Studies classes. When she told me, I dropped my books on the ground. My muscles forgot how to work.

We text and call Dee on and off for the next few hours, and when it hits nine and we still haven't heard from her, Whit is too restless to stay put. I tell her we can go check in with Madea, Dee's mom, to see if she's heard from her. Really, I just want to enlist some help that isn't my mom 'cause she'll stress heavy.

Mom returns quick and hands over the keys. She asks us to bring back some red beans and rice, Madea's signature, laughs, then is silent. I give her a hug and say I'll see what the universe tells us. She likes when I act mystical. In those moments, she thinks I'm smarter than I am.

I figure Dee might've trekked back to her childhood house. Hungover folks know how to find a friendly couch. After we get on the highway, I ask Whit where she thinks her mom would go. She says Dee's got too many people in Tacoma to really know. Then we are quiet for a while, and I start talking about jambalaya the same way I'd describe a woman's body. She calls me a fatty. She used to call Pops that too. We go silent again. The night is clear like most summer nights before August. I don't know what ghosts Tacoma holds for her, what corners and take-out spots can put her in the jail of memory.

My mom still has a house in Rhode Island, where I grew up, same state she ran away from Pops to. She dug out a life for us there—paycheck to paycheck, rental to rental, bailing out the sinking ship that was Pops' legacy. Now she's moved out of Pawtucket and has a fat mortgage. She's had some boyfriends. None could wake her up, except one that turned out to be racist. Naturally, that shit ceased. Her mom, my nonna, lived with us too, helping with the finances. She and Mom still live together, Nonna helping to pay a mortgage she never wanted. In time, I expect my mom will want the same, to move in with me. When the thought strikes, I wish I'd done something different with my life.

Every time I visit I drive home late, after the bars close, on city streets turned to soup by ocean fog, and I think about Whit and Dee. I don't know who needs more and who needs it first and if I even have it to give. I slow the car to a crawl and peer through the milky windshield—waiting for an emotional sucker punch.

DEE ISN'T AROUND, but Madea does want to feed us. Whit tries to stay in the car, but her cousins harass her until she gets out. Fred, Madea's second husband, Dee's step-pops, joins us. We crowd into the small kitchen to make plates. Whit takes only rice, none of the stewed tripe, pretending to be skinny—none of our kin is skinny. The kitchen smells like you could get spicy just standing in it. Her uncle Lenny, Dee's brother, and her cousins sit at the table too. I haven't seen them since the funeral. No one says grace. Whit doesn't bow her head to say a private prayer like Pops would've.

"You don't like the food?" Fred asks, mouth full.

"I'm not hungry," Whit says.

"Bullshit," Fred says.

"Leave her be," I say. If I'd popped one of the Percs, I'd be mellowed out. Instead, I fidget as Whit stares out at nothing.

"Tripe is good for the joints," Fred says.

I wonder if he knows that he's an idiot who doesn't make any damn sense. I wait for the "roots" talk.

Fred slurps the stewed tripe like noodles. "A man don't know his roots don't know hisself," he says.

"Be quiet," Madea says.

Fred inhales the fat. It goes straight to his brain. He's never liked Dee, who is a reminder of her pops, Madea's wild ex. When Fred would give her a hard time for being hungover, she'd say, *You just wish anything about you was hung.*

Lenny leans his paunchy, bald-headed self back and takes stock of my sister. "Looks like she eatin' fine to me," he says.

"Pookey!" Madea yells.

"What?" he says. "She don't look like no Make a Wish kid."

Whit clears her throat and glares at her uncle for a second. "Least I'm not bald," she says.

Lenny winks and goes back to work on his plate. Whit checks her phone below the table like a kid in class.

"Anyone hear from Dee?" I say.

The table goes silent. Madea's expression is tender, but I can tell she's mad.

"Ma put her out," Lenny says.

"Nobody is gonna threaten me in my house," Fred adds.

Madea gives him a look that could boil a potato. I don't know if it's 'cause the house is Madea's or because he's on one.

Whit tries to stone-face him too, but she can't and drops her eyes, pushes her plate away and crosses her arms.

"Threats?" I say.

Fred keeps eating. His face looks like a chocolate cream pie. It is just so fat. He tries to be gentler toward Whit. "A woman needs to eat, honey," he says. "No man like a scarecrow."

I am thinking about Dee and the words slip out before I can stop them. "You're fuckin' slow," I say.

Madea puts her silverware down. Fred keeps chewing, but deliberate. One of Whit's cousins laughs and Whit tries to keep a straight face.

"Just cruise the Way and she'll turn up," Lenny says. "She likes that place Brother's."

"I know this is a tough trip for you, boy," Fred says, coddling and demeaning all at once. I want to put a fist through his face. I stand to bus my plate instead. I take Whit's too and imagine slipping out to meet Dee, to get drunk and sleep in.

Madea finds me in the kitchen. "Fred talks a lot of noise," she says, "but Dee *was* acting crazy and I can't have that in my house. Not with the kids here." She turns the water in the sink on low so she can talk without being heard at the table. "She was falling asleep on herself and mumbling about shooting."

"Shooting what?" I ask.

Madea starts washing the dishes. She keeps the place plastic-over-the-furniture clean. "I don't know, just shooting. She wasn't making no sense."

"So you put her out?"

"I was worried about my babies," she says. "What choice did I have?"

I can think of a few but I know how steady she's been for her family and for how long.

"Giovanni, I've given that child all the love I can give her." She continues to wash dishes and I can tell she's going to tell me Dee's life story, the way moms do when their children have become strangers. "And the things she did to your father—"

Whit enters the kitchen and I'm spared. She sizes up the situation. "Start the car," I say, and hand her the keys. She hugs Madea and goes, happy to be gone.

"We'll find her," I say. I hug Madea too.

"You know that situation in Vegas is not what your father would've wanted—" Madea starts.

"Yeah." I step out of the hug and cut her off. She wants to get something in my head, but I'm tired of people putting my pops' dirty laundry on broadcast.

"Whitney always has a home here," Madea says, and the tone of it chills me.

On the stairs, walking toward the door, I give in—one pill, chewed quick to avoid the bitter taste. Since the moment I put them in my pocket, I was always going to.

BROTHER'S IS NEARLY empty when we get there. The eleven-thirty crowd on a Wednesday is weak. There is no sign of Dee. Some well-dressed white dudes sip brews slow. It is dark and the music is nothing I recognize. 'Cause of Whit's age, the bartender makes us take a table. Whit's shirt bulges when she sits. I watch to see if she fixes it or covers her stomach with a hand. She does neither and pulls out her phone.

I tell her what Madea said about Dee.

"Don't let Madea play you," she says. Whit's right about that, but it's also a deflection.

"What did your mom say about that girl Hannah?" I deflect too.

"She said black people don't kill themselves." Whit stares square at me. That sounds more like the Dee I know.

I go to the bar, order a beer and a Sprite, and ask the bartender about Dee, describe her.

"Yeah, she was here," he says, "calling all of us fims or something." He hands me the beer, then starts pouring the soda. "She's a loud one."

I ask him if he knows where she went and he shakes his head. Then I ask when she left.

"Do I look like her babysitter?" he says.

"You served her, though. She was drunk and you kept serving her, right?"

Whit motions for me to come sit down. As soon as my ass hits the seat, I take a large sip of my beer.

Whit starts typing on her phone. "What'd he say?" she asks.

"Your mom messaged me a minute ago." I take out my own phone and pretend to read a message. "She went back to the hotel," I lie.

Whit eases her body farther into the booth and takes an ice cube in her mouth. She looks again like the girl I used to push in the shopping cart at Target, way too big for it but smiling so wide, her eyes became accent marks. I'm not going to be the one to tell her to grow up, especially if she grows up to be like Dee or me.

"You want some cherries?" I know the answer already.

At the bar, my hand is in my pocket again, fingering another pill. I am pushing into that crescendo where you don't want the music to stop.

When I'm back at the booth, Whit picks up her phone again, swallows the cherry she's eating, and makes a call. From the register near the bar, Rihanna's voice breaks out, small and tinny: *Come here rude boy, boy, is you big enough…*

I laugh until I see Whit's face has gone blank.

"You liar," she says to me. She gets up and starts for the register.

I call her name. She speaks to the bartender and he hands over a cell phone.

"Whitney!" I say, sounding like my pops.

She walks right past me and heads for the door, then turns around and holds up the phone the bartender gave her. "Mom couldn't have reached you," she says. She is outside before I move an inch.

Pops was the glue. Without him, I can't imagine us finding anything worth building together. Whit speaks in hyperbole—"Oh my God, slit my wrists now," or "Just drown me." I give her speeches about debasing the English language, but she says some funny shit too, like calling white girls *mayonnaise inhalers*. She puts ranch on everything, though, like Pops used to. I don't tell her that ranch dressing is mostly mayo. Instead I laugh with her and point out fat white people at the chain restaurants. They probably point right back at our black asses.

I write poems and rap with some local groups in Ithaca. Neither thing has made me any money and probably never will. Dee watches cop shows and goes clubbing. Our connection feels like

142

a list of facts rather than a family. I send Whit necklaces and funny cards for her birthday. She says "I love you" on the phone and in her thank-you notes and posts pictures of us together on her social-media accounts. She posts old pictures of us with Pops too. We are all living on his memory—Dee on the insurance money, Whit on the love, me on a legacy I don't fully understand. A Nigerian in my class back at Cornell said that Americans expect too much of their fathers. In the moment, I hated her for it. But even in death, we still are expecting salvation.

Over Thanksgiving break, when I picked Whit up from school, she paraded me around to meet her teachers. Really, she wanted all the people she had beef with to see her giant brother. I told her I wasn't going to stare down a bunch of ninth-graders, but when I saw the way they turned their noses up at her and called her Juwanna Mann, I roasted them, telling them they couldn't even model for Braille catalogs so stop the cute shit and read a book. I wanted to love her like a brother should.

OUTSIDE, THE BROTHER's parking lot is empty and I yell Whit's name a few times, fake angry like I yell at my students. Then I get angry for real. It's an hour until last call, but searching bars isn't going to find Dee. Whit knows the city and as Dee's kid is no dummy, but I can't get past the images of her getting harassed by a pervert. Throughout that week in Vegas, I saw strangers leer at her the same way I leered at women alien to me—without a filter. I could've been in a hundred fights that week.

If I call my mom, her anxiety will flare up, and then I'll panic and that won't solve shit. I call Whit a few times but she ignores the calls. I think about yelling in a voice mail that her mom could be in the hospital, or dead, or arrested, but I don't want to put that in the universe. I'm walking fast down the ave., rationalizing—there is no way Dee brought her gun to Washington. She wouldn't pay to check a bag. I toy with the pills in my pocket, pinching the plastic. My hands are sticky and cold.

My mom calls and I ignore it. She'll call again. Her life is something you could set a clock to. The last time I was back in RI, I came in so late that she was up already. She grabbed me before I could make it down the hall to my room. I recited some poetry to set her at ease—*Don't be afraid, the gunfire is only the sound of people trying to live a little longer.* She asked me why I loved the poem so much. I was waterlogged from killing myself slow and didn't have much to offer. The next day, before she went to work, she left a printed copy of the poem on the kitchen counter next to the note she wrote every day. The notes were always filled with things she wanted me to do around the house, regrouting tiles and cleaning gutters, moving small shrubs or stones, simple things. I wondered what she'd found in the poem, if she'd found any of herself in those lines or if, like my nonna, she thought I was simply a sad man without a reason.

When Whit visited, they baked together and invented recipes. My mom showed her how to make pizzelles. Whit liked using the pizzelle iron.

I take out my phone to call my mom, then stop. Think about calling the cops, but I never have and never will. The image of Whit wandering alone almost makes me reconsider.

"Hey."

I turn.

"Take me to Silver's," Whit says.

I want to give her the whole "don't you ever" speech, but I'm not Pops and I'm fucked up—in no state to talk. "What's Sil—"

But Whit is already walking back toward the parking lot.

In the car, she looks straight ahead like she can see through the night into the past. I think I might see it too and finally give in and sneak a second pill from my pocket, chew it slow, blind to the taste.

SILVER'S IS HAZE-FILLED. They don't even bother carding Whit at the door. The karaoke is ugly. Some college-age kids spill their hearts on the mic singing Creed or Bon Jovi. I don't really know if it is Bon Jovi because I know nothing about rock, but it sounds like something a singer named Bon Jovi would sing.

I try to take Whit in again through my newly gauzy world. People bump and shove and I pull her close.

"You see her?" she asks.

I lean down and tell her no. Nuzzle her a bit. She cringes. I dig my beard into her like Pops used to do to me but she shrugs me off.

"Stop," she says. She isn't the same girl I took to Build-a-Bear when she visited. But I'm not the same man either. I've betrayed her trust, maybe we were never that close. I'm a light-year away and drifting farther.

I survey the riffraff, search for Dee in the crowd shaking her bony body, swaying among the college kids while belting out *I will survive*. I imagine harmonizing. But there are only some regulars staring down the college crowd.

I can't shake what Whit said, the image of Dee crying. Her frail body shuddering. Whit will be lost to me forever if something happens to Dee tonight. This I know. She'll remember me getting high and drinking when we should've been searching. She'll remember me lying. My imagination gets desperate—Dee asleep on a sidewalk or holed up in a den somewhere, like the stories I've heard about how she and Pops used to do when Whit would be at Madea's for days. Dee told me once about a crackhead chick Pops used to hide out with in Everett when things were going south and he'd been on one. She's told me too many stories like this and too late for me to ever hear the other side. Sometimes I wonder how much of it Whit knows.

"Let's check the street," I say. "You know anywhere else she might be?"

"Like where?" she says.

"Around here. A house, maybe?"

She looks at me confused. If I say anything more, she'll get defensive. I want her mom to remain a champion and Pops to remain a kind old soul. I want her to believe anything that won't sink her.

Outside, we walk along Tacoma Way, scanning for the Mustang on sidewalks and in handicapped spots. Some cars pass, not too many pedestrians. We do a quarter-mile loop and come back on the other side. I'm tired and sit down on a bench across from Silver's.

Whit joins me but keeps her distance on the bench. She starts crying, silently, and I stare off, get drowsy.

Mom calls again. I want to answer but I'm too high. My voice will pinch and she'll hear it. The pills are doing their work on me. My neck is a Slinky and Whit's face becomes inverted as my head nods. Mom texts me *911*.

I slide an arm around Whit, but she springs up, walks away to make more calls. I put my face in my hands to try and steady the world. Dee and I always think we'll make it home. Even unconscious, we'll drive. My head gets heavier and my mouth feels numb. I feel good, flushed. I tell myself this is me. But the truth is I'm over-faded. I dry-heave.

Sliver's spews out the last-call victims, but I can still hear Whit between the voices. "Can you pick us up?" she says into the phone.

I catch up with her and pull the phone from her ear.

"It's Madea!" Whit yells.

"Bullshit." The screen shows LETTY.

"Your son's high," she yells.

The blood in my calves is heavy and slow.

"Hello!" I hear through the phone.

"I'm fine," I say.

We are both silent instead of acknowledging the lie.

"You're just like your father," Mom says.

I hang up. Whit is smirking at me and I want to shatter her phone. But the Percs close in on me and settle me down. "Don't put this shit on me," I say to her, even though she has every right to. "That's your fucking mom, not me. I'm here." Even as I say it, I feel pathetic. "I'm here," I repeat, because it feels better than the truth.

My mom calls my phone and I turn it off. I shake my head to clear my mind and breathe in the cool, crisp air. The old drunks in front of Perry's, a bar across the way, are still smoking cigarettes and hanging around. Dee tried quitting a few times, but I know she'll burn until her face looks like it's made of chiseled oak.

"Get in the car," I tell Whit.

Her eyes are heavy, but she listens.

The stars are out, bright enough to see even in the city. I love Washington for that. I don't blame my mom for changing her tune after Pops' death, smoothing over his inadequacies. I've eulogized his memory too. I don't blame her for her nerves either. She's right, my life needs correcting. It's a little clearer now, after sorting through Pops' papers, the names on the check stubs like a hood genealogy test. I don't want my memory to ring the same.

As I drive, I pray for real, try to remember the Serenity Prayer that I read off Pops' NA books. It's a simple one, but I still can't find the words, can't fake the feeling that was real for my pops and our aunts and cousins who lived by it. Still, I pray—a long and undisturbed sleep would be worth it.

"You got a problem," Whit says. And she's right, but she's only saying it 'cause she doesn't want to think about her mom. Then she is crying. If you can watch someone you love crumble without crying yourself, you need to look for someone new because it ain't real. That sounds like something my aunts would say, but about soulmates. I wonder if the same goes for siblings. But you can't exchange blood.

It's hard to remember how to get back to the unit so I drive slow. Everything I have is focused on the road.

I remember when Whit called last Christmas. I was with my girl Madie's family. Whit said we should get to know our Big Momma before it was too late. We'd missed our chance with Big Daddy, and I'd missed mine with Pops. I wanted to tell her that I just needed to know that we'd be okay. Back in the other room, my girl's family was huddled together near their piano and a Christmas tree bigger than any I'd ever seen before—so big it must've been a twelve-footer. I told Whit she was right and that I was proud of her. We made plans to take Big Momma out for her eighty-fifth. But I never came through on them. Months passed and we let the gaps grow wider.

The storage complex is dark when we arrive, rows and rows

of units—a miniature city of material lives. I pull up and park so that the headlights show on Pops' unit, which is open, with an empty wooden folding chair sitting out front.

We get out and look for Dee. I call her name, then again, get mad and yell louder. After a minute of this, Whit collapses on a sofa that's been dragged out and lets the tears go. The Baccarat almost slides off the sofa. I catch it just in time and set it down inside the unit. Dee must've been holding it, a vestige of Pops' life before her, or maybe my mom came back and was remembering the life she can't seem to move past. I keep poking around, afraid to look at Whit. There is a metal trash can filled with a bunch of things half burnt. I call Whit twice because she can't hear me over her own tears. She rises off the sofa like she is fifty years older. I turn on my phone for the flashlight. We start sifting through the can.

Dee must have been burning things—pictures and papers mostly, the huge binder of check stubs, a couple of old Kodak disposable cameras. The smell of melted plastic is harsh.

Whit pulls out a soot-stained pair of panties.

"What the fuck?" I say and start laughing, hoping they weren't my mom's. I take them from her.

"What's wrong with you?" she says.

I turn the phone flashlight up higher and find a half-burnt letter addressed to Pops.

Dear Lonnie,

In case you haul off and finna forget where you rest your head, I'm sending you a snack for the road.

It's signed *Deandra Campbell*. There is more but I double over.

"What's so funny?" Whit asks.

"Pops and I had more in common than I thought," I say, and hold the panties up.

"Gross," she says.

A flashlight comes on in the distance.

I stop smiling and steel up. "Ay," I yell out.

When the figure holding the flashlight gets closer he lowers it so it doesn't shine in our eyes. It's Big Al.

"What do you want?" Whit's voice surprises me. It's got grit.

"I got a call from security," Al says. "A complaint about loud music playing and the smell of something burning."

It's 3:30 by now, but I think Al's full of shit.

"I was gonna call the cops," he says, "but didn't want to deal with the paperwork. Came down and she was dancing like a madwoman, throwing shit in the can, looked like a séance. She's been sitting in the office. No phone. Can't remember a damn number. She's lucky I came when I did. Had a bottle of kerosene not six feet away. She coulda blown her ass to Timbuktu."

Whit starts laughing so hard she's crying again.

"You people are fucking nuts," Al says.

"Shut up, fluffernutter gut!" Whit yells.

Big Al looks down at his stomach.

I burst out laughing like I'm traveling back in time. Whit's her mother's child. She can deal.

The nausea from the pills smacks me hard again. I put one hand on my chest and focus on breathing, in through my nose and out through my mouth. The panties, part white and part discolored from the fire, hang from my other hand like a meager peace offering.

EVERYTHING IS FLAMMABLE

Rye and I didn't talk much after I left Pawtucket, but he'd mentioned firefighting before so I wasn't surprised. I tried to keep tabs on him through Marissa Sr., his girl, and my mom. After I went off to college, I stopped coming around much. Aside from a quick stint living back in the city with my old girl Madie, I was a ghost—nine years a stranger.

In all that time, I watched him cycle through his life. First it was police academy. He'd been on the other side so long he was already half trained. Nobody wants to be a cop, I told him. After he failed the officer exam, he tried for export work but ended up shoveling snow for the city. Then it was corrections officer. Nobody wants to spend their days in prison, even if they get to go home at night. I told him if he'd failed one test he'd fuck up the other. He said I wouldn't make it in prison. I'd grow a beard and take steroids, I said. Let your degrees keep you warm, he said.

We spoke just after his daughter was born. He had named her Marissa Jr. to keep things simple but wanted to name her Minnijean, after a girl from the Little Rock Nine who'd dumped her chili on a racist white boy. He liked the nickname Mini. His lady wasn't with it.

He went on to tell me about his scores on the firefighter physical aptitude test. They made me proud. I imagined Rye climbing all those steps again and again until the PAT officers told him he had done enough.

As he spoke, his words bled and rippled into my memories of us. I couldn't shake the image of us taking the SATs in a cold room at the community college. He'd kept his stuffed parka on and had fallen asleep halfway through. The whole way home he talked shit about how great his NFL combine numbers would be. I told him college comes before the league, but he just laughed and made me stop for pastelitos.

I could see the PAT officers watching him maneuver the ladder like it was a small woman. He worked the hose with ease, hitching and unhitching it with speed. The rubber mallet seemed to swing down from his hand like it had a life of its own, moving the sliding weight almost a foot every time he made contact. The plate leapt as he struck. He finished so fast—eight seconds—that the officers forgot to look at the clock. The physical stuff was all light work for him.

Even with fucked-up SATs he'd still managed to get a full ride to Morehead State, in Kentucky. I remembered how he kept lying to my mom after he blew his scholarship. He had been working at the PriceRite for a whole semester before she came in to shop and saw him bagging groceries. She called me after that and asked if we'd been in touch. Last I'd heard from him, he'd said Kentucky was on some redneck shit. I lied and told her we'd been keeping up. I should've asked him more about how he was holding. In the summers, when I was home from school, we still lifted and balled together. I used to give Rye the business in one-on-one and we'd gamble until he lost enough to want to throw hands. We'd end up slap-boxing like always, but I could see his life was in a real hurry. He was getting into some heavy weight, nothing like the little dime bags we fucked around with as kids. He said he had "diversified." He smiled a lot less. He'd never talked much, but he'd gotten even quieter.

The PAT people must've wondered if the dummy for the drag drill had somehow gotten lighter. Rye pulled it with so much strength that he lifted the rubber feet off the ground. The ceiling wasn't low enough to make him really hunch—burning rafters might, buildings collapsing in piles of their own histories might make him duck, but the practice course didn't. He said the ankle weights they used to simulate boots were lighter than Timbs.

After I finished at Cornell, I stayed in Ithaca. I toyed with some fine-arts programs abroad, leaned on new connections, tried not to fall back to earth and wake up in my old bedroom. Over the phone Rye and I still talked about training programs. We understood lifting—moving the immovable until we were too tired to move it another inch.

The final firefighter PAT asks fighters to simulate tearing down walls and ceilings with a pike pole. It calls for endurance. Rye took to it, pulling and pushing in rhythm, moving the suspended metal weights again and again. He was gasping when the officers called time, but even though his shirt was fastened to him and his breath wavered, he refused to hunch over.

On the phone, I congratulated him on his baby girl because both our fathers hadn't been shit and he'd be a good one. He was well cut for fatherhood—I remembered him on the block all those years ago, keeping watch in case the cops came through, his stash behind a loose brick in a wall on Beverage Hill where I'd gotten head for the first time. He always looked so focused and in control.

The PAT officers had to tell him to let go of the pulley. His lungs begged for breath, but he still wouldn't hunch over. The benefits of working for the city were too sweet to give in, the comforts he could provide too good—space to breathe in a wide room with the NBA playing on TV, a crib with gentle wood edges, a flame-resistant wool mattress courtesy of my mom, Baby Jordans in pink and purple smaller than a fist. He'd be able to come home and keep coming home. The Marissas would know his footsteps on the porch, the same every time—a wolf's howl, calling, and Rye returning with some food to break and share. Simple hopes. He thought he could be on the right side of things for a change. He was never the type to pitch for the rush. He hated being one wrong move away from ten years. Ten years is a lot of life. Ten years would mean coming out to a different child, a child he had no part of—it meant being our fathers. He thought firefighting was his last chance for stable. And it was time for stable. But a fireman's hours were just as bad as being on the corner, maybe just as dangerous.

After the PAT we didn't talk much. When we did get up, it was about music and people from around the way, about women and who was still balling—conversations that slowly burned to the roach. Our language was breaking.

IN EARLY MAY, right after Rye graduated recruit school at the department, Marissa called from a cookout my aunt had thrown them. Her voice was creaky on the phone, and she wasn't the creaky type. We'd been family since high school, since she and Rye had gotten together. When I heard her gushing, I smiled, looking out my kitchen window onto an overgrown field in Ithaca. The white noise of the insects dropped out for a second and all I heard was her repeating *best of this city*, and *pride and honor*, words that weren't thrown our way often when we were young. She told me how official Rye was all decked out in his uniform, feeling as good as he looked—on the right side of things. He walked steady when the deputy called his name. His gaze was clear. He'd always been welcome in my mom's house because of that gaze and now he'd have the career to match. The Marissas were dressed up in the crowd. The baby in virgin white with a little bow, Sr. in something floral, looking sexy as the day that they made the little one, so proud of her man that they'd be at it again almost before the reception was over. My mom snapped pictures. She'd mailed me a few. I'd intended to get them framed but they'd gotten lost in the stacks of books and papers crowding my place.

Rye didn't think of the product he had left to move. That part of his life was smoldering. Instead, his mind was on the fire station he used to run by when he was still training for football—the men in their academy T-shirts, hosing the engines down outside, the whole day shining like it was nickel-plated. That's what he wanted his Marissas to see too.

Then, a few weeks into being a probie, Rye turned up at my friend Blake's, where I was crashing. Blake and I were sitting on his family's penthouse terrace in Manhattan when the doorman called up and asked if Blake knew a Rydell James. I thought it was a joke. I'd texted Rye the address when he said he was coming through New York but figured he was bullshitting.

"What the fuck are you doing here?" I said, smiling, when he got off the elevator.

He looked healthy, leaned out a bit. Rye pulled a bottle of

pills from his backpack with a wad of twenties rolled like a news-paper.

"C'mon, man." I sucked my teeth.

"Same shit."

"And why do you roll your money like the Declaration of Independence?"

He ignored me and we walked onto the patio, staring out over the rooftops that dotted Midtown with Babylon gardens.

"So this is how you're living now?" he said.

"I don't own it," I said.

"No shit. When you coming back to reality?"

"When I find a job," I said.

"I got some work for you." He lifted the backpack.

"Funny. I'm not built for that anymore," I said.

"Anymore? Nigga, you *never* were."

He tapped the top of his bag so it shook like a rattle. We didn't need to recap my corny attempts to get in the game.

"How's my goddaughter?" I asked.

"Good, man. Shit's crazy."

"You get the Js I sent?" I hadn't been able to find the grape Jordan Vs in a small enough size but figured she'd grow into them.

Rye was watching the sun set behind the skyscrapers when Blake came back out with beers. "This place is crazy," Rye said.

"Thanks," Blake said.

"I never met a black man named Blake," Rye said.

"Well, that's my name," Blake said.

The sun dropped completely out of sight, leaving only an orange strip diffused by the haze of the city. We drank our beers.

"You never answered me," I said.

"Jersey is crazy for this shit," he said. "But it's all Stars and Stripes after this."

"After what?" Blake asked.

Rye took the blues from his bag again.

"My 'rents are home," Blake said.

Rye tucked them back in the bag. He leaned over and slapped my shoulder. "I remember when you used to sound like that— *My mom's home, my mom's home.*"

"Fuck you," I said.

"You don't know me," Blake said.

"Yeah, this nigga always got jokes." I tried to defuse shit before it could heat up. I thought back to the first night we ever picked up, the way Rye searched the street up and down for cops. Not nervous, just vigilant.

"I heard there was a stranger in my house," Mr. Holland said, stepping out the door all of a sudden. He wore a beige robe and had a clear plastic cup in hand. It was 6:00 p.m.

Rye sized him up quick, then stood, and I took a deep breath. "This place is real nice," he said.

"As long as I've been working, it better be," Mr. Holland said and held out his hand. "I'm Blake."

I pictured Rye rolling on the terrace laughing at the name. *Like for real—Blake One and Two?* Giovanni and Blake. All we needed was a Winslow.

"Rydell," he said. They shook hands.

Mr. Holland pulled out a chair and sat with us on the terrace. He didn't take small sips like the refined man he was. I waited for the wisdom. He was known for drinking whiskey and dropping knowledge about civil rights and carving out your own space. None of that liberal, kumbaya bullshit. And none of that Marcus Garvey give-us-our-own-rock talk. I wanted Rye to be impressed by him the way I was.

Mr. Holland asked how we knew each other.

"Grew up together," I said.

"Went to high school together," Rye said.

The can felt warm in my hands.

Mr. Holland could sense the heat in the comment but only nodded.

Blake and Rye stared at each other. It didn't shock me that Rye cashed in on his courage again and again. Even in a place like this. I'd watched him do it enough growing up.

"Be a better host," Mr. Holland said, and glared at his son.

Blake looked at his pops, then away.

"And don't bring trouble in my house," Mr. H said to Rye.

I waited for Rye to say something out-of-pocket but he stayed silent.

Mr. Holland stood up. "Good to see you, Gio." He smiled. "And nice to meet you, Rydell." He began to walk toward the sliding glass doors. "Oh, and you know there are women in this city, right?" He laughed his way into the house.

Minutes later, Blake got up and looked Rye over. Even seated, Rye's frame cast a cannonball shadow.

"Who you mugging?" Rye said. "Sit your ass down."

"You better talk to him," Blake said to me.

Rye stood, but Blake stayed put a few yards from him.

"Aight, *Blake*," Rye said.

I stepped in the middle. Rye inched closer and I had to lean my weight into him. "Really?" I said.

He had the same level look I'd seen before. His phone rang

and he let it go. He still had the same ringtone from high school, J. R. Writer.

"You're a niggerish motherfucker, huh?" Blake said.

Rye kept his chin up, but his eyes widened. We knew the Kool-Aid.

Blake retreated a few steps toward the door, then spoke again. "Do you even know where you are?" he said.

Rye checked his phone and let the sliding glass door close behind Blake without saying anything.

"Fuck was that?"

Rye threw his beer can off the balcony and sat back down. "What?" He read a text and put his phone down.

Lights glowed in the windows around Midtown.

"You still serving Jason?" I nodded toward his phone sitting on the table.

"Money's money," he said. Jason was a regular.

We were silent for a bit.

"Fuck's wrong with you?" I said again.

"Don't talk tough."

"I'm not," I said. "I'm just trying to introduce you to—"

"You the fucking president?"

I glanced at the door. "You know you gotta go now, right?"

"'Cause of that candy-ass nigga?" Rye said.

He didn't move and my face felt hot.

"He's my boy," I said. My voice came out too light. I waited for the glass door to open. I imagined Blake's pops walking out and Rye flipping the table and swinging on him without warning. Just whaling on the old man. I saw the headline: "Prominent International Lawyer Assaulted in His Own Home." I saw the call he put in at Phillips prep school evaporating into thin air, undone by an appearance of family. I pushed the memories of Rye backing my ass up out of my mind.

I must've looked like I shit myself 'cause Rye broke into that I'm-fucking-with-you smile and laughed. "Take it easy," he said, and tapped me on the chest.

"I'm cool," I said. Down below, a mob of pedestrians crossed in front of the sandwich shop on Fifty-Fourth and Second. "Why are you fucking with pills anyway?"

"Lotta money in PKs." Rye spat off the balcony. "Kids ain't cheap."

"Way to be a stereotype," I said.

Rye got up and started for the front door without a word. He didn't yell or break anything. A courtesy. Near the door there was a picture of Blake's pops standing next to Nelson Mandela on a podium somewhere. Rye took in the picture, then turned back to me.

"For real?" he said.

"Crazy, right?"

Rye paused, taking it all in like he was coming into my world of wonder.

"He knows Morgan Freeman?" he said.

I thought about correcting him. I didn't. A courtesy.

"Come check me out soon," he said. "I'll show you the station."

"Yeah, for sure."

I dapped him up and he was gone.

A FEW WEEKS after I saw Rye in New York, my mom called to tell me about the Hazards' fire. Stovetop turned serious. Oil and water don't mix.

It happened on Rye's shift, his first fire. I imagined him in his gear, sweating in front of the smoldering structure, a three-family home that looked as if some blaze-toothed mammoth had taken to ripping the place down but had tired or eaten its fill and moved on. Too much smoke came from the hole for Rye to see the remains.

Rye was outside, adjusting the salvage covers in his hands. We'd known the Hazards forever. Down the sidewalk, Rhonda stood holding her baby. Dre Hazard draped an arm across his mother's shoulder and Rye turned his eyes away from it all.

"BC!" Babe yelled from the doorway.

Rye was thankful for the abbreviation. "Beige Cloud" was a shitty nickname, an image like a cartoon fart or Pig-Pen's dusty ass. In a city of Portuguese and Boricuas, he clung to his blackness like a damned Panther. He hadn't even been out on a call yet to earn his own, but nicknames were thrown at all probies.

The second floor drooped, disemboweled, and Rye couldn't block out the baby crying.

Lieutenant Moss came out the front door, down to where Rye was on the sidewalk, and clapped him on the chest. "What if this was active?"

Rye imagined the house in flames and felt himself shrinking away from it, freezing.

"The fuck were you waiting for?" The lieutenant pulled his mask off—his skin hung like the fur on a pug's face. "We need those covers." Moss grabbed the tarps from Rye's hold. "Does this look like a goddamned bachelorette party?" Moss kept barking.

Rye envisioned the weak spots on Moss's jaw, below the ears and the soft neck under.

"Strike one." Moss spat. "Probies don't last long if they're slow."

Moss reentered the building. Rye pulled his own mask down to protect his lungs. Sousa, another fireman on the crew, told him, the gear, wear it, always. Then Rye relaxed his shoulders in the face of duty like only a man of service can do.

"Please cover the crib," Rhonda said.

Rye didn't turn, held his breath, and followed Moss into the home.

Back at the station, after the salvage operation at the Hazards', the rest of his shift passed uneventful. I imagine the next morning he washed the engine until it gleamed, raised the flags, put the dishes away in the new wooden cupboards that closed sloppy, a hack job the city was supposed to fix, and then forgot to put on coffee for the incoming crew.

Moss cussed Rye out again and he put the coffee on, then walked out calm, trying to keep his job.

Babe caught him in the hall. "Whoa, Cloud Man, why so stormy?"

"Fuck the cute shit," Rye said.

Babe was two hundred and forty pounds. They used to call him Ox until he said his dimples made him too pretty to be an ox, so they took to calling him Babe.

"Moss fucking with you?"

"I'm just tired," Rye said.

"You know he just wants you out before the vote."

"I'm doing everything by the book, man," Rye said.

"Moss is a motherfucker. But it's all family. Take your lumps."

"Yeah, but damn."

Babe looked him dead in the eye. "Moss is just an old fuck," he said. Rye turned back and Babe lowered his voice. "He's over the hill—busted-ass knees and shit, flat feet, pumped full of Lipitor, inhaler puffing, hay-fever stricken, peeing twenty times a night, prostate big as a beach ball, Dick Cheney heart having. That motherfucker is the Life Alert spokesman." Rye cracked a smile. Babe winked and headed down the hall.

Rye watched him all the way into the kitchen. From around the corner, he heard his voice—"Hey, Cap! Fabulous morning!"

Rye missed being his own boss. I'd never seen him take shit, probably why he got fired so often. We laughed about the first few jobs because they were bullshit anyway, like the nursing-home security gig, where he got fired for inviting our boys to use the Ping-Pong table in the lounge, and then from the PriceRite for ringing up all the produce as green peppers 'cause he didn't want to look it up.

I'd told him sometimes you just had to kiss ass and play by the rules. That's how I'd gotten an offer from Phillips Prep, north of Boston, ground zero for ass-kissing.

In the car after his shift, Rye sighed and checked his phone. He had another text from Jason. He said he'd pay two dollars a milligram for some Perc 30s, and he wanted a lot. Jason even had that sucker hair that fell in his eyes, which were made for crying, too round and wet. He said "brother" and "fam," and Rye pictured his daughter growing up to pour chocolate milk all over a lame like Jason. I didn't like the motherfucker either. He used trust-fund money to get high. He played lacrosse.

MARISSA'S CALLS BECAME more frequent after Rye started at the station. She was worried about his double life. She couldn't understand why he kept at it. All I could think about was when Rye was first getting his weight up. We were seniors in high school. He would grab the front of my shirt and twist it in his fist like those white mobsters in the movies. Then he'd sing *These penitentiary chaaances that I take. Should be able to get the maaaaansion by the lake.* I would push him off and tell him to stop fucking around. That's when he loved to pull his money out. He'd smell the stack, thick as a textbook, and ask me about my AP classes, stressing the words like an asshole. He said money was freedom. He had plans.

DURING OUR PHONE calls, Marissa would ask about me, but her heart was never in it. Even if I wanted to, I couldn't give her much about Rye. We had stopped talking after he popped up at Blake's.

I still picture him coming home late the morning after his first call at the Hazards'. Jr. cried and kept crying. Marissa Sr.'s mom said that the baby had an ear infection and needed her head held up vertical.

"Take her," Marissa said to Rye. "She hardly slept last night."

Rye wanted a nap. He didn't sleep well at the station. He took Jr. in his arms and tried to maneuver the putty gently, always afraid of hurting her. In pictures Marissa sent me, Jr. looked like chewed caramel in his arms. They lay down awhile in the room Marissa and Rye were staying in. Sr.'s mom insisted they stay until Jr. got old enough to sleep through the night. Rye wanted them to get their own place. He positioned himself so that his chest was angled enough to prevent Marissa Jr.'s ear from hurting, but she carried on. He tried peekaboo and the smile game, which consisted of him smiling until he felt like an idiot and stopped. He flipped on *SportsCenter* and Jr. kept crying.

"You gotta help me with her!" Rye yelled.

Sr. entered the room. "Help you?" she said.

"I don't know how to do this. I'm trying, baby, really... Where's your mom—"

"My mom has seen more of your child than you have."

"I'm exhausted, Cocoa."

"I have to study," she said.

"I just got home."

"Well, figure it out," she said, and left.

Rye tried tilting Jr. this way and that to make her comfortable, but she screamed on. He bounced her on his knee and played rocket ship and wondered where the hell all her air was coming from. He contemplated walking into the family room and just handing her to Sr., but then he thought of the Hazards' baby boy wrapped happy and tight, safe and at peace despite the fire that had torn down the life around him. Rye rocked and rocked Jr. as she wailed. The Not Top Ten came on and he laughed at the bloopers.

"That coulda been Daddy," he said and pointed to the football highlights as a player dropped the ball a yard before the end zone to celebrate early. "Well, not the whole acting-a-fool part," he said, and Marissa Jr. burped loud, giggle-hiccupped, and started laughing.

As they were falling asleep, Jason called. Rye shook his head—fiending, he thought. He looked at his baby girl with her pursed lips like she was trying to blow bubbles. He ignored the call and then they both fell asleep like wolves in a den. They slept past lunch.

Rye woke up and slid Jr. gently off him. The room was bright and she was still sound asleep. The collections of a life were loud in the light—mobiles for the baby, his sneakers toothbrush-cleaned fresh and set in neat rows, Marissa's nursing-school study guides hurricaned across the floor; clothes, clean, dirty, and questionable, a fuzz-covered binkie, some cords tangled like vines. He managed to reach the closet, stepping carefully, and searched it for the shoe box that had no shoes. He swept the weed crumbs to weigh out a few bags, took some of the smaller nugs to weigh out a few slices, then opened a fresh QP and weighed out two ounces for some up-and-comers. He packed a bowl from the dregs and hit it while Jr. slept. It felt like she was so close. The room felt like a fucking shoe box. Everything was cramped with junk. He texted Jason back. *Gimme a week.*

"She could break her neck," Marissa Sr. said, in the room all at once. She kept her voice down. "She could fall and die and you don't even give a fuck. All you had to do is put her in her crib."

"She's asleep," Rye said.

"Babies roll." She picked Jr. up gently and left the room before he could respond.

He knew better than to argue his case, it would only make things worse. The bed was soft and hot where they'd been lying together. Before he knew it, he was knocked out again.

When he woke the second time, Rye stared out the window into the orange of the street lamps, heated that he had slept so long. He took the bowl from the night table and hit it until it was resin. The lights hummed like hives. He imagined the electric boxes sparking and setting everything in the room ablaze.

Rye slid on his Jordan 11s—they were lucky, the Monster Jams—threw his work into a backpack, then walked slow down the stairs. Marissa was in the kitchen, tight-faced and ready to fight. He poured a cup of coffee from the maker, which was still hot, and unplugged it.

"You're so fucking stupid sometimes." Marissa moved slightly in the doorway, cocking her hip. "You burnt?"

"I put out the fires, baby. I don't start 'em."

Marissa sucked her teeth. "Cornball." She tossed him a packet of sugar stolen from the 7-Eleven.

Rye mixed it into his coffee, stirring with his finger until it got too hot. He checked the stove burners. They were caked with oil. "Your mom cook again?"

"Yeah, you want some rice?"

Rye took out a sponge and degreaser and began scrubbing. After a few minutes, he ran his finger along the metal to check. Then he went into the living room and put his hand on each outlet.

Sr. followed him in. "Stop," she said.

He looked up.

"You're high," she said.

Still, he made his way around the room, inspecting cords for frays and rodent teeth marks. Sr.'s laptop was burning up. He shut it down.

"What the fuck, Rydell! I didn't save my lab."

"You shouldn't let it get that hot," he said.

"How long are you gonna do this shit?" She walked to him, took his arm. "Please."

A deep rumble started in the kitchen.

"What's that?" he said.

"It's just the fridge."

Rye pushed her out of his path and pulled the fridge away from the wall. He clocked the dust buildup, handfuls of gray dust balls near the wall. He swept and swept, using his hand like a broom, stretching his arm as far as he could, then yanking the fridge to get farther back.

"Stop!" Sr. said.

"You gotta clean this shit!" he said. "The paint is oil-based, the insulation is cellulose. The house would go up in a second."

Sr. tried to rub his back but he left into her mom's room. She was sleeping. He used his fingers to poke at her ashtray to see if any embers remained. She stirred, but she was fast asleep, unaware. The ambient sound of waves washed gently from her CD player. The window open. The night still. He took a deep breath and listened to the hum of the street lamp. After a minute, he walked back into the kitchen.

Sr. watched him, leaned back with her palms against the counter. "Deep breaths," she said.

He went to kiss her, but then just stuck his index fingers in her ears. She shrugged him off. He turned to go, grabbed the bag with the work.

"You're really gonna leave like that?" she said.

Rye stood with his arms around her, then kissed her forehead. They held each other a moment longer.

"This isn't forever," she said.

"This isn't forever," he said.

"Don't let them kill you," she said.

"It's just weed," he said.

"And fire," she said.

She kissed his Adam's apple. He flinched.

JASON HARASSED RYE for a week about the PKs, and the morning Rye was able to set his hands on them, Jason was MIA. Rye texted a few times, even called. No answer. Rye was due at the station by eight. I imagine even he started sweating. Shit got hectic. His car idled in a parking lot looking out at Newport

Ave., which would take him to Rumford or the station, depending on the turn. He'd left the Marissas early so he'd have time to drop the pills at Jason's. He called Jason and called again. Waited and called again. The clock slid and slid again—7:00, and 7:15, and 7:30. *Ten minutes early is twenty minutes late*—the damn recruit-school lessons echoed in his brain like a PSA. A good probationary officer would've been at the station by 7:30 the latest.

"What the fuck, dude?" Jason said. "It's seven thirty in the morning."

"I need to drop these off," Rye said. He held the pills in his hands, the whole script wrapped in cellophane. The weight stunningly light, each pill so small. The sun already shone bright over the Episcopal church sandwiched between gas stations. People paraded in and out with coffees and an easiness that clean lives can give. The sun had only been up for two hours and he was already sweating bricks.

"Drop it off later," Jason said.

"I got work," Rye said.

"You're a drug dealer."

Rye put the car in reverse. "I'm headed your way," he said.

"I don't have the dough."

"Get it."

"I'm hungover, dude. Come tomorrow."

Rye had begun to hate holding the prescription shit more and more. Class E felony. He hung up. It was almost eight.

MARISSA HIT ME up that morning, stressing heavy. I tried to tell her that I hadn't heard from Rye in a while. I didn't mention New York.

"You should call more," she said. "He talks about you." She

asked me again about Rye dealing and about my life and if I'd liked Berlin. I'd been to Russia earlier in the summer, but I didn't correct her. I'd been visiting my friend Aimes from college. He taught over there. The Nevsky Institute had offered me a job for the following summer. I didn't mention any of this. I asked how her classes were going and about my goddaughter. She eventually said that Rye was bringing home more money now. She asked me if he was getting into powder and I told her she was crazy. She was right—just had the wrong drug.

I felt her anxiety over the phone. A teakettle whistled in the background, followed by some bangs and clicks—cup, kettle, stove.

"You wouldn't tell me shit anyway," she said.

I assured her I knew nothing. I actually wanted to ask a lot more, but that would've been admitting I was a godfather in name only—in reality a ghost who had to imagine them living and loving in that space, trying to put armor on a life that couldn't be protected.

"I been around," I said.

"We haven't heard from you." Her voice flat.

"I saw—" I almost slipped and told her about New York. "By the way, if you fuck up drawing my blood," I said, "I'll revoke my godfather status."

"If I ever get certified," she said.

"Ni puha, ni pera," I dropped some Russian on her.

She laughed and it sounded like she was blowing on her tea to cool it. She didn't even ask me what it meant. "Come by soon," she said.

After she hung up, I thought about when Rye had called and asked if I'd be Jr.'s godfather, one of a few. The offer felt like a bullet in my hands. I liked the weight of it because it felt solid, one last promise. I'd sent cards and presents, but those things were easy.

MOSS SAT IN the firehouse kitchen that morning as Rye crossed through to throw his things in the locker.

"Strike two," Moss said. "You're late."

"Sorry, family drama."

"Shoulda picked a different one, then."

Rye wanted to crack him across the jaw but jammed his hands in his pockets, surprised to feel the work there, the whole bundle. He willed himself not to look down.

Moss stared at him like he was an alien, then walked away.

Rye couldn't believe he'd forgotten to leave the 30s in the car—$4,800 of work bulging out of his pockets. Everything became an alarm. He wanted to go back to the parking lot right then, throw the pills in the console. But he kept hearing sirens in the stillness—boots on tile, the station TV, the bass of a stereo, a cell phone, the microwave going off, the dispatch, another cell. He couldn't risk being the last one to the engine. He shoved the pills into his locker but kept wanting to go back. Moss watched everything.

The day hit the highest temp of the summer—104. The city ran on faulty window-unit ACs. He sweat silently all day until Babe asked him to lift in the afternoon.

Moss came over to heckle him as he worked. "If only you could save lives in the weight room, huh?" he said.

RYE USED TO jab me like that, but always with love. He'd say shit about me being soft to piss me off, then slap me on the chest when I'd show and prove. Afterward, he'd come back to my mom's, where there was no government cheese, and she'd make white-meat chicken. He'd dig in the fridge for bologna or hot dogs instead. He did like her meat gravy, though, with the meatballs and sausage. He'd eat bowlfuls of that while my mom smiled because being a mother has always been her calling.

One time, after we ate, we went back down to the park to shoot around. He rolled a dutch and we sparked. He was always careful to keep his smoking weed away from his selling weed. He even picked it up separately. He was weird like that. It was hot and the park was almost empty. We got so high we couldn't even finish our game of horse. We sat on the metal bleachers with our shirts off, looking up into the haze of city sky. Some people milled around him for bags, and he broke them off.

"How much you making?" I asked him.

He smiled. "Enough to eat," he said.

I told him I wanted in. And I did, and had tried, stuck between visions of my life—what the city expected us to do, deadbeat dad, same old jazz bullshit.

"Nigga, you don't need in. Your moms feeds you." He threw the ball with one hand at the hoop and it ricocheted off the side of the backboard. "Imagine my fucking mom in the kitchen? The woman can't even boil water. You got a backyard. Your mom's a teacher. You eat grilled chicken for dinner. She's gonna help you go to school and leave and never come back." His eyes were far off like he was envisioning those things for himself or his family.

"You're family too," I said.

But he still was looking off like he could see through a wormhole into the future or an alternative universe where we'd known each other only in passing, a cousin you'd walk by on the street even though you used to be in the tub together, wanting to get the water when it was hot, before it got dirty, and find a spot on the bed before your sweating cousins pushed you off.

"Leave. Don't stop," he said, his eyes still on the horizon, above the leaning homes.

RYE'S SECOND FIRE was one street over from my mom's. She said she could smell the smoke. It was a two-alarm. It came in the sleep of night when fires tend to spring like resurging dreams, hot and hungry, turning acquired lives to ash, leaving nothing behind to truly measure the people who made the space a home— a necklace, perhaps, the gut pipes of a house, useless to all but investigators, who never knew the victims but construct a story for those who wish to know, maybe insurance, able to pick only a silhouette from the wreckage. That's how I feel now.

The city was a tinderbox of old homes, sloping and dry, with old electrical and too many people doing too many things in too many outlets. Rye outfitted himself in under two minutes. Found his spot in the backseat of the truck. They were stretched thin and put him on forcible entry, his first ever. Sousa drove with Moss beside him, more silent than usual. Babe got situated last, next to Rye in the back, no dimples. The other engine loaded up too. They called that crew Benfica 'cause they flew the soccer club's flags in their lockers. Rye's crew left the station and he prayed for the first time since Jr.'s christening.

The fire was on the east side of the city, on Cottage Street, a longer drive from the station. The houses were mostly one-family there, but still packed in so the shades stayed closed. Cars lined both sides of the road, fitted tight like molars.

Rye picked out the houses of people we knew—Hess with the blue eyes, and little Ricky who wore kid-size Jordans even in high school, and the Katzoff family who cooked a stinking sausage on Fridays that no one could ever find in the city. I hadn't talked to any of them since I'd left. Rye held each memory as it roared past. Each unlit house passed like a breath, life-giving.

They turned onto Waterman. From a distance, it was just the smell.

Moss started yelling, "It's go time, boys! Locked and loaded!"

"Showtime!" Babe said. He reached over and clapped Rye on the back.

The men kept hollering, but Rye remained silent. He thought the house would look like a jack-o'-lantern, surrounded by crowds and pity and something more sinister. Back before Rye had a family to build and a home to keep, we used to set off cheap fireworks on a street down at Slater Park, watching the weak lights trail into the sky. Rye thought about Jr. trapped inside. His knee started bouncing. People littered the road, huddled together with loved ones, hoping theirs wouldn't catch next. The smoke came in billows now and flames could be seen through the windows. The horn blared and people cleared, some slower than others. Above it all, streetlights still cooked. Then something else caught and the flames rose higher. Rye gripped the handle on the side of the truck tighter, tried to steady himself, battle every fiber in him that screamed, *Flee!*

He ran over the details of his mother-in-law's home—the medicinal smell; the matchstick rooms in the back, all wood-floored; curling irons; a cigarette left burning, maybe; the candles she lit sometimes when she drank her wine and listened to Aventura; old Christmas lights plugged in too long; an overloaded outlet. He knew their accumulated lives were begging for fire.

The horn sounded again and the people scattered on a street that Rye and I had walked dozens of times to Black's for pancakes and thick-cut bacon.

The smoke came clouded in deep hits, obscuring sections of the house as they pulled up close as they could on the curb. Benfica started rigging the hoses. I wonder if Rye prayed for his Marissas.

"Get the fuck out of the road!" Moss yelled. "Jesus."

Sousa pulled the air-horn cord to blow on top of the sirens.

"We got a job!" Babe yelled. He bounced in his seat.

The smoke was getting thicker. Rye gripped his mask and dismounted swift. He made sure the face piece was tight. The hook felt clumsy in his hands. Moss bounded ahead. The front door stood wide open. Babe searched the outside to read the extent of the fire. Sousa worked the hose.

A woman yelled something to Moss about her husband. "He went back—" Her voice trailed off as Rye and Moss approached the house. The heat intensified and the air thickened, toxic and sharp. Rye froze.

NOT LONG AFTER Blake's, I decided to take Rye up on his offer to check out the station. I hadn't lied when I told Marissa that I'd been around. I stopped by my mom's place first to pick up some kids' books. She put some cake in a Tupperware for me to give to them too. Seeing Rye with Jr. made her heart full, she said, shuffling around the deck, her spine curved like a question mark. Her garden was lush with flowers. I told her she needed help with the house. She turned to me with her dirt-caked gloves, smiled, and waved me off.

I swung by a bookstore to pick something special out for Jr., but the covers were all white faces or dragons. I figured my mom's gifts would be enough.

Dunnell Park was still filled with people playing ball or just sitting on the benches talking shit and smoking Blacks. The old backboards had been replaced by beautiful Plexiglas ones with air pockets that were supposed to make the balls bounce truer. The parks in the city had always been beautiful.

Outside Marissa's mom's place, people came and went. It was one of those days so clear that the sky blue seems to magnify everything, not bright enough to make you squint but enough light so that everyone is outlined in gold. I parked and gathered the books onto my lap. I left the cake. The windows in front were too small to see if anyone was home. A few people dipped past, too young to not be in school. Everyone looked so young— I couldn't pick out a single face.

A man near my age came down the block. Even from a distance, I knew it had to be Dre Hazard. The Hazards all have these pretty features about them—big, rounded eyes and a strut that's a little too light for a man. He had grown a beard. An ease broke out inside my body. I wondered if he got in any games these days. The books slid awkwardly in my arms as I rose out of the car. The parking job didn't leave much room to get through to the sidewalk. I had to turn sideways to pass by. I smiled as I stepped toward him. He drew level with the car and slowed down. A book dropped from my arms to the ground. My height made it difficult to scoop it up. As I stood to ask him how he'd been, I saw him clearly. His face was foreign. We stared at each other for a second. I nodded. Got nothing in return. He continued on.

I sat down on the hood of my car for a while, put the stack next to me, wanting to be caught by someone I knew. A few people passed, but folks weren't congregating like usual. The tiny front windows of Marissa's mom's spot remained dark behind the glass. I put the books on the porch and left without ringing the bell.

ALL RYE'S FOOTBALL weight slammed through the door. He couldn't see more than a yard in front of him. His undershirt was already soaked. It took him a little time to steady the can, which felt heavier than usual. Rye and Moss surveyed what they could of the front room. Nothing. They listened for screams. A TV lay smashed on the floor. The heat must have melted the mount. The seconds burned away. Fire danced around the walls, growing, mesmerizing. Rye couldn't tell if the broken vases and plates on the floor were from a rapid exit or from the blaze eating through their lives.

Moss looked and looked again, quickly moving through the room. He shouted to see if the trapped man could answer his voice, but the flames rushed like air through a subway tunnel. Moss yelled at Rye, but Rye couldn't hear so he just screamed, "What?" His suit was swamped. Moss's face was blurred. Rye waited for heroics, anything. He thought Moss pointed down a small hallway into the back rooms, but this was a shitty version of two-in-and-two-out—one in and two outside. Rye was going in alone. There was too much heat. He wouldn't make it out. Flames rolled along the ceilings. Turn-back type flames. Every step crunched beneath his boots. His brain worked quicker than it ever had. Fear made him dexterous but his vision was all but gone.

Moss came up next to him, got the can vertical, and aimed the nozzle in front of them to cool their path for the search. They couldn't see well enough to read each other. There were two doors, one straight ahead and one on the left. Orange billows licked around the edges of both. Rye realized he might have to use the Halligan. Again, Moss pointed him into the blaze.

Rye thought he heard a voice come from the back room. He followed it to the rear, maneuvered the sledge toward the door straight ahead, but the smoke made him dizzy. Even behind the visor's tint, he felt like he was staring straight at the sun. He crouched and tried to find the handle to open the door, reverting to instinct instead of training. It was stuck and he scrambled to turn back. Moss stood behind him in the hall. Something else caught in the house and exploded like napalm. Rye thought the whole place was coming down. Neither of them could scream loud enough to be understood. Rye took shallow breaths, worried about his air pack, then leaned all of his weight back, raised his tree trunk of a leg, and busted through the door with his boot. Something had caught inside. It was too hot for him to move anymore. He lay flat on the ground, paralyzed. He thought to crawl. Moss had made a mistake. They should've waited for the water.

Babe's voice bellowed deep enough to be heard behind the home. Rye lost sight of the doorway. He tilted his head back but could no longer see through the flames. Moss would come for him. He started hallucinating—picture frames melted like candle wax on the dresser. A man cried, huddled in a ball by the windowsill, which was also ablaze. The flames from the mattress roared deep, curling all the way to the ceiling, also newly caught, the temperature somehow still rising. He inched toward the man, who danced like the flames. Rye turned his head to find the exit. Everything was spinning. He looked back once more and it was a woman this time. He couldn't will himself to move.

The fire tore at him, seeped inside him. He thought his gear was failing. Even amid the heat, he tried to get up to a crouch but couldn't bring himself to. At last he lay flat and used his elbows to pull himself forward. All the walls were burning now. He shut his eyes tight. He could feel the solid handle of the hook against his thigh as he crawled. He thought about smashing his way out, but he knew it was a fantasy. Suffocating, he let his thoughts run away—a beautiful woman he should marry, the mother of his child, his child, a felony worth of pills. He didn't want that to be what his family remembered. The ceiling began to sag, ready to collapse.

Still flat on his stomach, he realized he'd never find the doorway. He rose on numb legs to a crouch. His eyes opened once more, swept the room once more. Everything was lit. Then the water came.

Outside, the woman stifled her cries for a long time, occasionally choking loudly. Moss tried to rest his hand on her but she shook and shook.

Rye, half conscious, couldn't look her in the eye. "There was no one," he kept saying, even though the words were weak in his throat. The house still smoked.

Rye's eyes stung. Babe stood a few feet away. Moss took statements. Sirens took the night. Babe should've pawed Rye like a cub or said something, but he knew that it wasn't the time. Rye smoldered, the pain yet to set in. He crossed himself once and thought about the pills that were still in his locker at the station.

He hoped they would let him clear his own shit out. As they pulled him onto a stretcher, he prayed again that the Marissas were sleeping soundly.

In her message later, Marissa said that Rye kept repeating that he couldn't find anyone, over and over, like he'd developed a tic. She said 5 percent of his body was burnt. He was laid up. She asked me to come see him. The messages from my mom said it was all over Channel 6.

When I got Marissa's message, I told myself I'd call back. A few weeks later, I picked up the paper and saw that firefighter Sean Fernandez had died in a different city at a different time. I read the whole article. He had dreamed of being an NFL running back. The captain called him effervescent.

The whole world felt preemptive. I never even checked to see if they'd gotten the books.

The night of the Cottage Street fire, a body was pulled from the gutted home, burnt beyond recognition.

DRESS CODE

Simone Perez had grown into a woman men called out to relentless on the street. She told some of the stories to her man, L, about visiting her family back in DR and sidestepping out of trouble like she had shady-nigga radar.

So one day when she was out walking on Newbury and three men, one of them with a clipboard, approached her, she didn't cuss them out or put her head down and walk faster. She paused, ready to roast them. They asked if she'd like to be part of a photo shoot. She laughed in their faces and asked how stupid they thought she was. Then a short dude with an accent took out a black binder and opened it. There were pages upon pages of photos, photos of his paintings. The packed ave., corner store, parade crowd had all been caught in motion, in a moment where life vibrated to the surface and couldn't be suffocated. He made the world seem like it was posing. Those were only the stills. When she got to the portraits, she noticed they were all men, all black, all in control—of themselves and, in that moment, perhaps, the world around them. The eyes in the paintings were dead set at the viewers, daring them to try and take anything else. She wanted that.

Once upon a time, L had had that look about him, but she'd gone to take premed science classes at Gordon, a Jesuit college up north of Boston in the countryside, and he had stayed put and slowly worn down. When she came back he was different, but she couldn't forget the first L.

The man with the accent seemed to be made of wires beneath his clothes. His tight woven scarf, peacoat, and leather boots were curiously clean. Above all, he had an official-looking clipboard. He reminded her of the creative-arts majors at Gordon. While she studied the work, he explained that there would be a meet-and-greet. Dressmakers from the top fashion houses would fit her and all that. Some of the top photographers would take pictures. Then he would turn their work into portraits. Her mind slipped away. When her mom had been healthy, she used to make all Simone's clothes. The girls at her school would ask where the clothes came from and she never told. The man with the accent said her dress would be stitched to her exact dimensions.

It sounded like game. She tried not to look impressed—to convince herself this was nothing special. As the spring breeze blew some cool across their bodies, she asked why he'd picked her.

"Self-possession," the man said. He took out his card, Brandt Cameron, and wrote his personal cell number on the back.

FIVE MONTHS PRIOR, L had quit his job as an electrician's apprentice. When he'd started, he kept saying the money would get good, but she'd heard him bitch often enough about lugging cables across roofs for eleven bucks an hour while his toes froze in his boots to know he would quit before he did.

The first few months after he put on some weight. She offered to pay for some classes at CC, but instead he got a job telemarketing cheap home-security systems. He didn't feel good about the minor panic he caused customers on a daily basis, but he was coming up quick on thirty and needed work. Since college Simone had been treading water as a secretary at an architecture firm—scholarships to dental school were few and far between— but for the third year, she was preparing to take her DAT.

L had been there since before, when she had braces and carried her sketches of *Le Petit Prince*. Back in high school, when the world was getting ahead of him, when he was making schemes about his future as a music-video producer and mogul, she had tried to rein him in, give him steps, get him to think about college, finance, business management, anything more tangible.

DUB'S BOSS, SYLVESTER, had given them all types of ways to tap into people's fear. In his heart of hearts, Dub knew most of the ways were suspect but couldn't pass up the possibility of a 20 percent commission. Most people just cussed him out. Some creatively, like the guy who said he hoped Dub became dyslexic and could never read a phone book again. Nights at work were seldom good.

But despite having moved into a shoe-box apartment after a couple lean months, on the day he and Mone visited the house on Parkside Ave., Dub pretended he wasn't dead broke. The real-estate agent had gotten there early. He could tell by the way the spot smelled like scented candles—cinnamon rolls. She wore business clothes and smiled a lot. Her teeth were large. Dub didn't really like women in suits. He thought it made them look like dykes. He wasn't used to dealing with real-estate agents, just with landlords who hated their jobs, some who carried heavy wrenches because their tenants had loose definitions of "the first."

Mone kept her eyes low, but he could tell by the way she shook her head at the small flaws—worn linoleum in the kitchen, missing bars in the banister, the weathered porch—that she really loved the place. If she hadn't, she'd have been more polite for wasting the woman's time. At the first place they'd visited, the agent had gotten out of a cleaning van still in her sweats and T-shirt. After trying the wrong keys a few times, she opened the door to a cross between a litter box and an ashtray. Mone had been polite, respecting the woman's hustle. Now her rudeness was apparent. She loved the house. He thought of his younger brother Nick's new spot, almost twice the price and in Lincoln, of all places, near a damned country club. Dub didn't like quiet neighborhoods. He didn't want Nick's life either. Still, he couldn't deny Nick's place was nice. It had all sorts of space, plus a pool in back. Dub paused in the family room of the Parkside house. The carpet was dingy—no stains, just worn down.

Simone listened to L downplay the house at every turn—*I thought the yard would be bigger. The kitchen linoleum needs to be replaced. Is the water pressure always like this?* Easy fixes, really, but she could see him doing the math in his head. He'd been doing the math since he'd left his apprentice job. Nothing was good enough, even though she knew he was running out of money fast. He put money in the wrong places. He still bought new sneakers as soon as they came out and wanted to take her around to clubs. She thought they were both too old for that, but she'd always relent and smile because he'd say, *You look so good, I gotta show you off.*

She imagined what he'd think of Cameron's work, how it might look over the fireplace if they could, by some miracle, move in here. Cameron's offer sprang up in her mind like it'd

been coiling there for days. She wondered if he'd found someone else to paint. She knew enough to know the house was a
stretch, at least at $197K, and that was after all the mortgage-
application costs. It was damn near impossible. She remembered
the way her Gordon friends rattled off names—Caravaggio,
Cézanne, Vrubel—ivory-sounding names. She knew that a
Brandt Cameron would never land in a place like this. She
thought of how her white girlfriends sent nudes to their
boyfriends and then got mad when their men shared them with
their friends. And now she had a chance to be made into royalty
on a canvas. She chose to believe the world was finally laying op-
portunities at her feet.

They waited till they crossed back over Newport to speak.

"You can't even see the river," Dub said as he came to a stop
at York.

"Did you see that backyard, though?"

"That ratty-ass patch of grass?"

Simone cut her eyes at him. They neared his apartment,
where the houses atrophied like they were sick with something
incurable. But only a few streets north stood a pocket of homes
so clean, it felt fake. In high school, Dub would borrow his boy
Rolls' car to drive her out near the lake in Slater Park to fool
around. Pawtucket could surprise you. Or sometimes, during
free periods, they would just wander up Denver Street, where
he'd point to the houses and ask which one she wanted when he
went to the league.

She was too religious to actually get down and too smart to
pretend Dub wasn't talking to other girls. She knew he liked that
she was the class president and liked how the teachers took him
more seriously when they saw them walking together. And she

liked being smarter than him. She felt their relationship could never get out of hand that way.

"You follow up on that maintenance offer?" Simone turned onto his street and imagined him in the reflective vests, hopping out the truck and using his hands to fix the city. She hated to admit it, but she liked that he was mechanical. It was manly.

"I got a job," he said.

ON THE WAY home, Simone stopped to get takeout for her folks— pork chops, rice and beans. She hated picking up things she could cook herself, but her mom was having another episode with her MS, and El Paisa was her favorite. She pushed that out of her mind and focused on the smells from the bag, and the Supremes bumping from the speakers. After a minute she got sick of the idea of love lost and shut off the stereo, listening instead to the wind through the open windows.

After her parents were fed and on the couch watching Yankees' spring training, she dug in her purse to find Cameron's card. His website was beautiful, the background floral and simple. There were links to galleries he'd exhibited in around the globe. She felt awoken, not starstruck. She looked through the photos slowly, taking in the sheen on the skin, the faces, some famous. Did people actually buy these? She read the dimensions and wondered how the hell they fit in homes. Maybe they'd wind up in museums someday.

Cameron had a high voice—said he was glad she called. Of course he remembered her, said she wouldn't regret this, then gave her a time and place. She'd have to get to Boston in two days. She was too caught up to ask any questions and felt dumb on the phone. It was an alien feeling.

After the conversation, she kept scrolling through the pictures, studying the posture of the people. The paintings were saturated in grace and decadence. The kind that would sink a normal home. She imagined them scrubbed down, then painted over, the way they did the murals near her aunt's in Olneyville. There was no need to look in the mirror. She knew how to pose. She and Dub had gone through a few honeymoon phases over the years, and when things were good, he liked to make her lie on the bed after they were done. She never let him take real pictures, but he would make a box with his fingers and pretend he was snapping shots wildly. She'd tell him to stop but mean the opposite. Sometimes she was tempted to actually let him snap one, something just for him. Not something forever like the Cameron paintings. Now she imagined floods in the glass galleries, the colors of Cameron's work running together until every one of the paintings was bloated and mud-colored.

A DAY LATER, Simone stopped by L's before he went to work. She thought maybe the shoot could get both their minds off the house, stop the falling feeling. When he said no before she even finished the question, she pulled up the website on her phone.

Dub remembered a girl they used to go to high school with who got caught up in some shit like that. Now there was a video of her on the internet with over a hundred thousand views on a site Mone would've been disgusted by. He'd known a lot of girls who got passed around, neighborhood property. Mone had a good head on her shoulders, though—she wasn't the type.

She sat up from the small armchair and slapped his foot, which hung off the bed. The midday sun shone bright through the worn curtains. It looked like an apartment with cats in it, but he had none.

He moved his foot back onto the bed and continued to look at her phone, peering up to see what his girl's face looked like.

"What do you get for it?" he said. He handed back the phone and picked up a *Ring* magazine. It was filled with flyweights he'd never heard of. No one cared about flyweights. They didn't hit hard enough. Everyone wanted to see knockouts. Dub was the type to talk shit in the barbershop, like if he ate healthy and jumped enough rope for a month, he could be a heavyweight contender.

"I didn't ask," she said. "How about being excited for me?"

"Slave labor." He pointed to a picture in the magazine. "At least they get paid for their work."

Simone looked out the window. The woman next door was picking cigarette butts out of the small flower beds on the sides of her steps.

Dub caught her staring off, concentrated on her eyes. The ceiling slanted behind her, bright and backlit from the light outside. It was late-spring warm. She looked good in her yellow dress. He wanted to peel it like a banana, and sat up to tug the loose fabric.

She snatched it back and tilted her head away from him.

"Just don't expect too much," he said.

She eyed him up and down. "I never do," she said.

"Yeah, aight." He leaned forward, grabbed her under the arms, lifted her onto the narrow bed with him. He pulled her dress up and blew on her stomach like she was a trumpet. Her body shimmied like cold water touched it. They kissed and he sucked on her bottom lip, then leaned back to take her all in.

* * *

DUB HATED HAVING to wear a tie to a job where no one even saw your face. Plus, since his weight gain, he felt like Mone's fat little nephew, the one they called Albóndiga. He told himself the mirror at work made everyone look like shit. Still, he tried to smooth out the bunches in his shirt. If he could lose fifteen or twenty pounds, he might be able to model himself. Ha. He'd been out with Mone so many times when people laid weak game on her. He assumed that was just a young-woman thing. She wasn't a model either, not that she wasn't beautiful enough, but models didn't breathe the same air. They did juice cleanses and had purse dogs. Models from around the way ended up getting loud in beauty salons and going nowhere fast. Just like the old-heads down at Atomic talking about how they could've been on the Red Sox if they went to the batting cages more often.

Sylvester was on him about low sales. Despite wanting to spit on him, Dub knew he couldn't go another night without getting an appointment. He watched the evening sun fall, threw back a NoDoz, and put on his serious voice.

Mr. Airewele, do you know about the rising crime rates in your area? When unemployment goes up . . .

He tried to keep it factual, for the most part—sometimes even tried to keep it light.

Oh, you have dogs? Nothing some cheap steak and pepper spray can't solve, you—

But Sylvester said that jokes and charm didn't sell in this business. Dub knew as much, but these people were strangers. Whipping up hysteria seemed like a job for governments and news agencies.

He went into the break room to eat a few oranges. The manager came in so he pretended to be on the phone. When the manager was out of sight, he sat down and played with the peels.

His boss poked his head into the room again. "The most important call is the next one," he said.

Dub chewed the orange pieces slow. They were sweet and cleaned the taste of NoDoz off his tongue. He needed two appointments that night and he'd be back on track for his number. He remembered Mone running her hand along the mantel and looking out the sliding glass doors to the porch. The yard was nice. He could even put up a swing set if they had kids. He shoved the rest of the orange into his mouth and chugged some water to clear his head.

Mr. Johnson? The man had a gruff voice. Dub took a shot. *Are you aware that the Rhode Island gun laws aren't in any hurry to change? Oh, you own one yourself? Smart man. Do you sleep with that gun on your nightstand?*

Sylvester came into his periphery and gave him the thumbs-up. Once you passed thirty seconds on the line, the odds skyrocketed.

Dub felt sick, but a gun owner was already paranoid, he rationalized. *You don't? Well, do you know that, on average, it takes a determined criminal only seven seconds to reach your bedroom upon entry?* There was a silence. He knew it was the moment, didn't know if he could push it any further. *You're not the only man with a gun . . .*

ON THE MORNING of the shoot, Simone drove her mom home from the doctor before heading up to Boston. The doctor had put her on new medication. It was supposed to cut relapses in half. Simone had asked about side effects and who the manufacturer was. She distrusted American doctors. Her friend's mom in high school had gone home to visit relatives in Ecuador and came back with her lupus cured. Sometimes she thought the whole country revolved around keeping people sick. Orthodontics seemed clear-cut—straightening teeth, a service important but without hearts on the line. Plus, she could hook up cheap dental care on the low. She'd seen her dad fix cars in exchange for food or help putting up their deck or cheap plumbing. Sometimes he even fixed them for free.

She didn't tell her mom where she was headed, didn't want her to worry or question it. She'd come home with the pictures, maybe even a dress. She'd heard that sometimes models got to keep the clothes. She could store it away for when L finally asked her, or maybe she could sell it to help toward the down payment. She couldn't imagine what the dress would be worth. Then the paintings would come out and even if people had no idea who she was, they'd be awed by her likeness. Not the way her boss complimented her haircuts, with that smile that suggested something else.

When she arrived, the pitchers of water were filled with cucumber slices and mint leaves, and the light falling through the factory windows made the space look like a ballroom. She'd assumed all the old factory buildings in East Boston had been abandoned, but this was an oasis. Refurbished light fixtures hung from the ceiling in steel-cocoon blossoms. The place was sparsely furnished, but the floor was new. People whirled around wearing satchels and capes. Other women looked side-eyed at the whole affair. These were not the naive young women who made the news for being taken advantage of. These were not even the cocoa-butter ones who got snatched up as video vixens. These were women in their late twenties and thirties. Still, some of them scrambled through their bags looking for accessories or checking themselves in small flip mirrors, reawakening a dream in themselves like teenagers, a dream they'd thought long dead.

Simone didn't want L's dreams to dry up, just to age and mature. She was supportive, she just wanted him to be smart. In high school, he would convince his boy Rolls to borrow camcorders from his dad's store and charge kids at school to shoot their crappy music videos. Simone actually thought they were good with the camera, and L had the charisma to get girls in the video and knew enough people to fill out the flicks and make the rappers look tough when they weren't. Still, the end product was always grimy. Same as when L had done a short stint as a club promoter and even gelled his hair like a guido. She knew that the city maintenance job meant family benefits and guarantees. Who wouldn't back that? But he didn't want the life she did, or if he did, she couldn't always tell.

For her, the shoot existed outside all that. She let the space wash over her and took a break, took it in. The workers exuded fashion above the daily, not all flashy, but demanding a second glance. Some became new personas and switched bodies—men to women and back again. The clothes they wore made their fluidity clear. L would've said they looked like skinny-ass Prince lookalikes or some other stupid shit. If she had moved to Boston after school like her classmates, she wondered if she would have gained entry to this life. She tried to envision L stuffed into the poncho of the skinny man who was ushering her toward the woman taking measurements. The poncho probably would've made L blend in with the aging men out around the Transit Center wearing dresses and capes and belly shirts two sizes too small. She frowned.

"Not many lights," Simone said to the skinny man.

"Better contrast," he said. "Don't worry, your painting will look like prom-night photos on the world's best crack." The man left without introducing her to the woman measuring.

Simone didn't even register it, already transfixed by the dresses. They weren't all folds and lace like she'd expected. Some were simple, dark blues and shades of black, exposing radiant patches of shoulder. Some looked Grecian, the women dark-skinned beneath the white toga-cut dresses.

The woman eyed her closely and scanned the rack adjacent. She began holding different dresses against Simone. "Tall," she said.

Simone couldn't help but smile. She'd never been the slump-shouldered type. Some of the dresses had fishtails. Some were hemmed short. She couldn't stop staring at a charcoal one with blue hues, a dress she could wear out into the world without looking insane.

The woman followed Simone's eyes and pulled it off the rack. "This reads nice on your skin," she said. She began moving efficiently around Simone, measuring and pinning fabric back in places. It actually wasn't too different from the way her mother had measured her when she was little. The movements relaxed her.

It wasn't a cookout dress, but she could get away with it at a quinceañera, or maybe L would take her to Trinity Rep to see *Memphis*, though she knew he wouldn't. He hated musicals like her family hated Lucifer. She wanted to twirl and see the dress's angles in the mirror and had to check herself. She wasn't going to let a dress turn her into a child. Instead, she stood straight-backed in the mirror and smiled, slowly striking poses and realizing how natural it all felt.

* * *

DUB WOKE UP with the sun. He'd had nightmares about having to move in with Mone and her family and her dad snuffing him out on the couch. Her dad had never been a big fan. He didn't say it outright but he always spoke about what his nephews were doing. One even worked for Google. Dub wanted to throw shots at him for being an out-of-work mechanic, but Mone respected her father too much and he knew not to cross that line.

After two glasses of water and a clear piss, he tried to do the math. Without getting any commission, he could swing another month's rent. He knew Sylvester was just waiting to fire his ass, but he tried to put that out of his mind. All morning, he lounged around mad that he had the night shift again. Around lunch and after a nap, he heard steps on the stairs. The stairs were so shot they even made Mone sound like the police.

She'd brought the photos. For Dub, the snapshots looked too much like rich people's marriage pictures—people he and Mone could laugh at in the mall arguing over Pottery Barn shit, maybe his boy G's people. He tried to stay positive. Mone did look impressive in the dress, even though it was still a little baggy on her figure. He couldn't lie, he preferred her in booty shorts or black skirts with platforms, sundresses, or just panties and high heels. His memory was a distracting motherfucker. He liked Mone a lot of ways. The pictures were crisp, but he thought that any creative nigga could take a decent photo. If she wanted a photo shoot, he had boys who could do it.

Mone was excited to see what the test shots became. Dub looked at the gold hoop earrings she wore in the photo and couldn't stop thinking of the ones she used to wear with her name in the center, bought at the bodega where the case had a hundred names. He thought about the nonexistent money that'd been coming in from work lately, and the house seemed like a distant memory and the only way forward.

"They look aight," he said.

She frowned and held out another photo. "They're going to tailor the dress just for me."

Dub got up and started getting ready for work.

"No comment?" she said.

"I don't wanna watch you get played," he said.

She wanted to hit him. "Stop being ignorant."

He picked up her photos and threw them across the room. There was silence.

He looked at himself in the mirror, but only quickly, avoiding getting lost there. She was the reason he even had a high-school diploma. But the words came before he could stop himself. "Any dumb-ass with a camera can make you look good." His hands kept struggling with the buttons on his shirt and he felt old, too old, like he had missed his cue to change.

"Your dumb-ass friends?" she said.

"My friends? Your girls are fucking lames."

"Yeah, just like you," she said.

He stopped messing with his shirt. "Okay, *Miss Secretary*."

At least some of his boys had gone, left the city. Many hadn't. A few came back. Ty started a foundation for ball players to "end the violence." He still had the same big ears and deep voice. He didn't live here anymore. Dub didn't want to either. His brother had left. Dub liked the sounds of dogs barking and kids running around, but twenty-eight years in the city was too long.

Simone clenched her jaw. She'd swung on him once before. She'd broken lamps and flipped end tables. Now she simply collected the photos that were on the ground.

Dub became nervous. He was used to her cussing and fighting back. He felt the distance all at once. She wouldn't look at him.

"Mone!" He tried to make his voice cut but she only shook her head. She gathered her things and was gone before he could say anything else.

He spent the better part of an hour comparing his life to his boys', his brother's, shit he wasn't prone to. He'd always had a side hustle—hooking up his boy Gio with phones to sell when he went abroad, Mitchell & Ness jerseys back in the day, mix tapes, movies. Not that he was on a fast track to wealth, but he was never stationary. Now he couldn't even remember his last project. Nick had bought a house at twenty-five. Rolls was opening his own exhibits and making 60K doing graphic design for G-Tech. Dub couldn't even change the odds for his own girl. Outside the window, on the stoop across the street, some little kids in shirts three sizes too big were playing taps with a worn ball, throwing pass after no-look pass. The clock caught his eye and he realized he'd have to start walking to catch the bus.

Dub peeled and ate his oranges before he even picked up the phone to make his first call. His mom always told him to watch his blood sugar—fruits unfurl slow, burn low. She'd also told him never to eat Chinese food because it was prechopped, and prechopped chicken and prechopped seagull look real similar. He'd outgrown that one.

Sylvester came up behind him and rubbed his shoulders like an old friend. "How you feel, how you feel, how you feel?"

Dub shrugged his hands off. They weren't contact-close. "I feel like—" *Knocking you out* is what he thought. "Making some sales," he said.

"My man." Sylvester took the peels from the table and shot them into the trash like he was Paul Pierce pulling up from deep. "Bottoms!" he said.

Dub ran his hands over his head and realized he needed a cut bad.

Throughout the night, he went blank during calls and got hung up on before he could even get started. He felt nervous the way he used to before his big football games in high school. He thought about Mone standing in front of lights and being ogled, but then he thought about a different reality—her nervous and making herself small. He realized he never worried about her moving in the world, only about her moving away from him. He'd found himself a fighter and never questioned it, but when she didn't even care enough to yell, he was done for.

He imagined her with the fans blowing and cameras flashing and all the other model clichés. *Work it, doll. Lift your chin up. You're a lioness.* He imagined the room arrayed around her in that charcoal dress. There probably was a professional smoothie maker and stylists named things like Sky and Fuzz. All he could think of was a convention hall and people in chairs like it was the Oscars. He didn't know shit about a photo shoot. Then his mind switched quick and he thought of amateur porn videos where the whole flick was a setup and the women were bad actors. He thought of a girl from high school, panicked, and called his boy Rolls.

"What's good with you?" Rolls said.

Dub told him about the shoot and the house and work.

"I got tree."

"Nigga, I'm calling you from work," Dub said.

"Right." There was a long silence. "You ever think it could be legit? Mone's bad. Maybe she just lucked into this."

"Come on, now, how many girls we came up with actually end up modeling for real? Remember Bria?"

"Yeah, I seen the video."

Dub could hear Rolls sipping something on the other end. "You faded?" he asked.

"Trying." There was another pause. "You're acting real paranoid. You have to figure she's gonna get something out of it." Rolls sipped again.

"Yeah," Dub said. He searched his mind for something to say but there was nothing.

"One photo shoot isn't gonna make her leave you," Rolls said. "Maybe stop being an asshole."

"You're high," Dub said.

"But not wrong."

Dub heard the ice in the cup.

"Come through after work," Rolls told him.

THE DRESS FIT perfect. It didn't pinch or bunch anywhere. It moved with her, tight up top and draping below her waist like fancy curtains. She'd seen these types of dresses in the closets of some of her former classmates, smooth and stitched to suit their personalities. Cameron and his people had decided to rent out a warehouse in Chelsea, not far from the Tobin Bridge. She thought it was strange that the shoot was taking place so close to the hood, but then she remembered that artists always wanted to be *close*. She held on to her dress like it was money she'd found in her pocket. It slid with her hips like snakeskin. The seamstress had to pull her out of it, otherwise she would've worn it the whole day.

A pretty man named Manny did her makeup and hair. She was

disappointed that they straightened and curled it. They were turning her into a brown Princess Di.

"Do you like it?" Cameron asked Manny. He was posted in the doorway of the bathroom they'd annexed.

"Do *you* like it?" Manny repeated.

"You're going to call me Boss Man next," Cameron told Manny and let a cheap laugh go. "You look majestic," he said to Mone. He stepped back, looked again, then left the bathroom.

In the mirror, she watched as her hair was burnt into a bouquet. She couldn't stop thinking about the dress and hating herself for getting giddy. She thought about the clothes her mom made—uneven at the seams if you got close enough to notice.

IN THE CONFUSION after the shoot, Simone forgot to ask any questions. She'd expected Cameron to invite them all out, but dinner got delivered to the warehouse, vegetable quiche and tomato soup—good for their humors, according to a fecalist—and then all of a sudden, Cameron was no more. His assistants gave the models their reservation confirmations for the hotel and said Cameron'd be in touch about the exhibit date. It was going to be months later anyway. Simone took in all the info as if it weren't her being painted. She peered out the windows to be sure he was really gone, evaporated. She came from a long line of people who believed in ghosts and she started to doubt the whole event. As the rack of dresses got wheeled away, she managed to ask about their final resting places.

"They go back to the fashion houses," the assistant said. "They get altered for the runway."

"Right." Simone turned away from the woman, thankful she was too dark to show the blood in her face.

Hours later, at the Hilton she wished she'd just driven home. She lay on the bed in one of Dub's old shirts with her hands tucked inside, feeling the smooth of her stomach, pressing on her belly button until she felt the tingle in her gut that always made her shiver a bit. The TV was off and she kept the curtains closed because her room faced away from the skyline. She was alone with the questions she'd never asked—back at college, letting go of the connections she should have stayed in contact with and pressed for job interviews, and long before that, as a girl in seventh grade getting asked to join the mock trial team and swallowing the invitation down inside her, letting it die there, not wanting to argue with her parents about the value, having to pay for the trips, not even wanting to ask. Weekends were for church and housework.

She thought of Cameron in the studio with her images, transforming her into a woman who asked for things owed to her. She was still to be unveiled to the world. That was something to look forward to—some ceremony that would change her in the way she always thought a doctorate might. Doctors are never left behind. They are saluted in their own way. She had a lot of cousins who'd joined the Marines for less. She rolled over onto her stomach and fell asleep on top of the covers.

THE WAIT SET in. Dub had been the lowest-selling salesman two months in a row. Mone'd kept giving him rides to work the past few months even though she was silent the whole way. He'd ask about her DAT prep or her parents, his own form of apology. He could see there was something she wanted to tell him, but she said "Fine" and nothing else. At least she kept the routine, though. At the end of the third month, Sylvester told him he'd have no choice but to fire him if things stayed the same.

A few days later Mone said she couldn't take him to work. She gave no reason and hung up before Dub could press her. At the bus station, he sat next to a woman who needed sleep bad. Her eyes fluttered closed again and again. The 78 was behind schedule and he started to hate Mone. He knew she could withhold a lot of shit—sex, communication, whatever—but she was fucking with his job, the one thing she was always bitching at him to keep. She knew better. He didn't know if it was a final warning or if she had really stopped giving a fuck. The woman next to him smelled sweet, like lotion. He wondered where she was off to or coming home from. He loved the way Mone smelled when her perfume had time to mix with her sweat a little. The smell could make him cross-eyed even after all these years. That was something not to take for granted. He knew that. In a different life, they would settle down like his bro and his wife, in a suburb, have people over for parties. He tried to laugh at himself. What type of caged-bird shit was that? Maybe they'd met too early. Or maybe he'd just made the wrong moves, falling out with his connection in the mayor's office and messing up his in with the city, not taking Mone up on the classes so he could get his associate's—shit, not even staying in shape. He prodded his gut every day before putting his work clothes on. He tried to run a few times a week, but after a mile he'd stop and sit in Slater Park watching teenagers skip class to get high, same way he used to do.

The woman next to him had fallen full asleep. Her arms were crossed and she was mouth-breathing. The bus still hadn't showed and he was fucking heated that Mone hadn't given him a ride.

At work, his phone threats escalated as the hours passed—

It's a good neighborhood... for now.

You hear about that minister in CF?

Hello, Mara Silva? Is Raymond in? No? Well, do you know... And then Dub thought about what Sylvester would do. Dub's own mother slept with a lead pipe next to the bed ever since he and Nick had moved out. Shit, in his own kitchen he often thought of which pans could be used in a moment.

Does he work nights often?... Yeah, my mom was the same way growing up. He paused, having given something of himself. *It's nice having a full house.* He tried to be vague enough, heard her voice waver. *I had a brother. We kept each other company... Oh, I was calling—*He passed the thirty-second mark and Sylvester hovered behind his station. There were no cubicles. The idea was that watching other people make sales motivated the team. The team wins—the company wins. Bullshit, niggas just got jealous of one another and threw hate around in the lounge. *I'm following up on a system your husband ordered.* Silence. He let the lie linger. *Yeah, we spoke last week... Are we still on schedule for Friday? I could call back, but my manager is here.* He looked over at Sylvester, who mouthed *Don't let them hang up.* Dub added, *He said we could upgrade you to the premium for no charge. It covers everything.*

The line was silent. He thought of the news paranoia—opposite of the dream. They'd foreclosed on his mom's house. He later learned how common it was. He taught himself about predatory loans. They were the dream. Then the nightmare. After his family was moved out, some local artist painted a mural of *Jurassic Park* dinosaurs on it. Little kids still played make-believe games in front of it. No one tagged over it. It didn't sell.

Dub heard motion in the background. Sylvester held up a sign that said TALK UPGRADE. *We can upgrade you for no charge... Well, if he calls back, I don't know if my manager will be here…Of course I understand, I just don't want you to miss out. I'm trying to help you.* That's what they were taught. He softened his voice for *help.* You wanted the buyer to feel like a winner. Like they had a need. *I use Safeworks at my home.* He thought about how ridiculous he sounded, how much of a fucking liar he'd become. *My mother lives not two blocks from you and she sleeps with a pipe by her bedside. I know how tough it can be.* It was the truth but it felt heavy and awkward. *I understand that your husband is usually home, but criminals aren't stupid. They watch.* He took a deep breath. *They're sick people. They know your space, the layout of your home, your schedules, maybe even what you do for work.* He heard movement and thought she was hanging up. But the line didn't go dead. Was she looking out the window? He felt sick. Was she clocking the parked cars? Sylvester held his thumbs up and Dub had no choice. *I understand that, Mara, but I want you to think.* He paused for a second to think himself about how fears creep in from nowhere but then make themselves at home. *Do you really feel safe?*

DESPITE THE SALE, he was fired two weeks later. He couldn't bring himself to ask his boys for money. Instead, he asked Rolls if they needed any help in the shop, but Rolls' father said they couldn't afford it.

There was a silence.

"You good?" Rolls asked.

Dub said he was straight.

To make matters worse, the price on the Parkside house dropped. Dub desperately kept up appearances with Mone.

She called him after she scored in the ninetieth percentile on her dental-school admissions test. At first, he didn't know if it

was to gloat, but she wasn't the type. He finally breathed a little easier now that the freeze was over. They were having a real
conversation for the first time in months. He talked about the
improvements he would make on the house. She even agreed to
come over for a celebration dinner. With the last of his money, he
ordered their favorites from East Garden—General Tso's for him
and beef and broccoli for her, pork egg rolls for both. He worried
that the lights would be turned off in the middle of the meal.

She watched him struggle to eat. There was nothing in the
fridge, not even juice, and there was always juice. She didn't
know where they were headed, but she knew never to pry. He
was the type who would yell and walk out the door. It was hard
for her to keep a smile on her face. She felt fake. There was only
one light on in the whole apartment. They were looking at shad-
ows of one another.

Mone scheduled interviews at Howard and Mercy Detroit.
She scheduled them for weekends so she wouldn't miss work.
During the process, she lived off fast food and hardly saw L at
all, but she imagined him wasting away and knew her leaving
might leave him assed out. She got accepted to the Mercy pro-
gram the same week Cameron finally called and gave her the
date of the exhibition. L deserved to know. She called, but all
she could bring herself to do was invite him to the exhibition.

DUB FELT LIKE a clown, showing up to a red-carpet event unemployed, but he couldn't tell her as much. He had felt the distance
closing and thought of this as a chance to push it all back to good.
She wanted him on her arm and that was the most important
thing. She wasn't embarrassed by him, above him, leaving him in
the past. They'd put too many years into this thing of theirs. She

must've come to the same conclusion. He started thinking about this night as their unveiling rather than as an exhibit where Simone was one of many models. Somehow all those eyes would force them closer. What if the artist had made her look bad? He thought of having to comfort her. He imagined a skinny man in black with trendy glasses. He could have that type of man shitting himself. He also knew Mone would never forgive him if he started something. She'd told him long ago that testosterone only gets a man so far. But he'd never believed her. It's about money when you don't have it. It's a man's world.

Then, a few days before the exhibition, Dub came home to a thick orange envelope from the city. He didn't realize he was a whole two months late. He tried his kitchen sink anyway. No water came from the tap. He sat on the outside steps for a long while. He sat until his legs started to fall asleep before he decided to ask his younger brother for help. He called Nick, lied on the phone and said he wanted to check on them. Maye, Nick's wife, was pregnant. His bro told him not to come, but Dub said he'd already gotten the day off. It took him a while to find the right bus to Lincoln.

When Dub got there, Nick pushed open the door and turned back toward the kitchen. As Dub closed the door, he noticed it had no peephole.

The house smelled like lime and garlic. The rooms were clean—plastic-covered couch, religious shrines, scented candles.

"L," Maye said. She cut a slice of lime and held it out to him like it was normal to suck on limes. Even pregnant, Maye had a quick smile. It made you look away from her warped-barrel stomach. She wasn't glowing like women always said. She looked sluggish and weighed down, but still she smiled.

Dub took the lime and thanked her, all the while watching his brother move around the kitchen somewhat frantically. Nick slapped Maye's ass and kissed her on the cheek even though the force could've tipped her uneven frame. She smiled and went back to the stove. Dub chewed the lime slow.

"Baby, you seen my thick socks?" Nick asked, taking up the whole doorway in his pants and undershirt.

"You earn any mall-cop stripes?" Dub put his peel down.

Nick stared at his older brother. "Private security, bro," he said.

Maye's eyes bounced between them and she turned off the burner below the rice. It went out like a gasp.

"Tough guy, now, huh?" Dub said. It'd been more than a year since the wedding. Dub hadn't seen him all that often since then. His brother did seem more settled into his body.

"Laz, you look like you could eat. Would you like something?" Maye said.

Dub registered again how hungry he was and how good the food smelled.

Maye started putting some rice on a plate. "I don't cook the chicken until Nick gets home, but I could heat you up some leftovers."

"You're not going to eat before work?" Dub asked.

"I'm late."

"I came all the way out here—"

"I told you today wasn't good." Nick picked his black button-up shirt off the back of a kitchen chair.

"I need to talk to you," Dub said.

"Then come back this weekend."

"I need—"

"First day on the new contract, bro."

Maye was still near the fridge, but she was silent. The hum of the fridge became noticeable for a second. It was one of the stainless-steel types, military-looking.

"Nick," Dub said.

His brother turned, still in his undershirt. Maye was staring and Dub hated that it had to go down like this. He wasn't lazy. It shouldn't have to be this way. He remembered his coaches telling him to work smart, or work hard. Maybe he'd done neither.

Maye had her hand on the fridge and he couldn't help but think of what she might pull out to go with the rice—pork, maybe even steak caballo. Nick's girl could cook. Who knew how much food was in that mammoth fridge. Nick could eat. He and Maye were both homebodies. They were well suited that way. That's what it was all about, Dub thought—being well suited. So many weren't. Maye had blue nails and perfect cone fingers. They looked small wrapped around the handle of the fridge. There was probably fruit and ice cream and whole un-cooked chickens and juice and milk and ribs—

"What?" his brother said.

Dub turned away from the fridge. His brother had become a man, and this was his space.

"Don't waste my time, bro." Nick pulled his shirt on.

Maye ran water in the sink. The sound drowned the room. There was a window above the sink like in sitcom kitchens.

Dub started to hate their home. It was fake. At least he and Mone still went out, remained alive and not cooped up like an old white couple. Then he thought that maybe Mone just didn't think he was the right man to be cooped up with. She had loved the shitty little house. It wasn't shitty. He'd imagined sitting at the table with her and staring off out the sliding glass doors at the backyard.

"We gotta talk," Dub said.

"I gotta work," Nick said.

Maye pulled open the tank fridge and took out something wrapped in tinfoil. Dub thought back to when Nick would bring his friends to the party and jock him for introductions to older women or for weed or to buy him LQ. Dub couldn't believe he was being treated like a fucking bum. Maye put a bag of marinating chicken back in the fridge. Outside, the spring light dropped and outlined all the trees in soft dusk light.

"I need money," Dub said, still looking outside. He waited awhile before he turned to see his brother grinning.

ON THE AFTERNOON of the event, Simone showed up at L's to find him in a suit and tie already. Her stomach was knotted from putting her mom to bed after an MS flare-up, but the sight of L in a pastel purple tie and a black suit made her laugh. It would have worked if L was a sports anchor on ESPN.

"They're not those type of people," she said.

Dub wanted to get mad—he couldn't stand feeling dumb—but he took a few breaths through his nose. "So what type of people are they, then?" he said.

"First off, your coat is going to get wrinkled in the car," she said and slid him out of it, enjoying the width of his shoulders still, after all these years. "You should know that."

He wanted to tell her that this was the same suit he'd worn to his brother's wedding, but he didn't. He remembered the look on Nick's face when he wrote out the check a few days earlier. He wanted to tell her about that too, and for her to tell him that it was okay to ask for help. They hadn't been open like that lately.

She dug in his closet to find the only pair of formfitting pants he owned, which happened to be black jeans. "Here," she said, handing him the pants. "They're these type of people."

He held them up, wondering if they'd even fit. She undid his belt slow, then pushed her hand down over his dick. He caught a whiff of her perfume and jumped to attention. Sometimes he hated how she had that over him. Sometimes she would just exit the room and leave him that way.

She felt anxious and on top of the world all at once and she loosed it on him. When they were done, she helped him dress and rested her head on his shoulder, and they looked at themselves, their reflections not as old as they imagined.

THE GALLERY WAS all glass and angles, concrete floors and blank walls. The space was much larger than necessary for the dozen or so paintings, but it was twisting and there were rooms to slip in and out of. Simone dragged L this way and that. People approached her to shake hands and congratulate her as if she'd painted the portraits herself. The servers wore white shirts and dark ties. The wine tasted average. The fancy women guests wore collared shirts, hair pulled back. L smoothed out his untucked gray shirt beneath the jacket. His shoes felt tight in the toes. Mone pointed out Cameron. Dub thought Cameron was posing, all the people revolving around him. Dub wanted to chop it up with him.

Simone walked slow past the paintings, giving equal time to each, pretending she wasn't looking for herself. A few white people came up to her to say *What an honor* and *How fun*. Another tried to ask questions like a reporter—maybe she was about subverting expectations and breaking the mold. Out of the corner of her eye, Simone watched Cameron kissing some well-dressed people on the cheeks. She assumed they must be other artists or critics. L stood in front of one painting—a black woman decapitating a manly white woman—his hands stuffed into narrow pockets, letting the party swirl around him like fog. She wondered if they saw the portraits the same.

She came up behind him and whispered in his ear, "What do you see?"

He had been staring at the woman's hands—strong-looking hands. He tried to take the whole painting in, think of something smart to say. "What kind of fucking question is that?"

He let his hand drop to her ass and she smacked it away.

"Watch yourself," she said.

"Don't pretend you don't like it."

She stepped back and cut her eyes at him. The suit jacket from the wedding was a little too dressy for the jeans. "I know what you're trying to do." She focused back on the painting.

"Who are you trying to be?" The words were out before he could stop them, then Mone was gone. Some people approached her and she smiled like the sun was sitting in her lap, like he didn't matter.

CAMERON FOUND MONE studying a portrait of one of the models that he had painted from behind. The event was still buzzing, journalists and critics glad-handing.

"This isn't you," he said.

She wanted to suck her teeth at him for thinking as much. She knew it wasn't her, but she was daydreaming about where the paintings would wind up. A bald white man had said it would sell for a third of a million, almost enough to buy her dream house twice over. She wondered if they'd all sell for that much.

She watched L trying to button his jacket up as he approached them.

"Have you seen yours?" Cameron asked.

L froze on the edge of the conversation. Mone glanced at him. He waited to be introduced.

Mone tried to stay relaxed. Her body tensed up and she didn't know who she wanted to do right by. She calmed herself by cataloging their humanness. Cameron was short. Dub was reckless.

"You're mysterious," Cameron said.

She'd heard that a lot. Too many people took her silence and patience for mystery.

L brought his eyes this way and that, then stepped in front of his girl and stuck a hand forward. "I'm Lazarus, her fiancé," he said.

Simone coughed a little.

Cameron took Dub's hand slowly. "Biblical," he said.

Dub threw an arm around Mone in an awkward gesture. "It's not all that. She calls me L," he said, and tried to smile.

"That's nice," Cameron said.

"We're going to my portrait," she said.

"Oh, it's yours to keep?" Dub said. He looked directly at Cameron, who was silent. He waited for Cameron to fidget. He didn't.

A few people spotted Cameron and came to kiss the ring, sensed something, and waved instead.

After taking them down another corridor, Cameron turned to Simone. "Here."

The painting was in its own alcove. Almost three feet by two feet. The likeness was impressive. Dub focused on the lips and eyes. Cameron got them right. Mone's skin was church-smooth, like Sundays before service. Her head was slightly cocked, chin held to the side. The eyes got to you. He wondered how long it had taken Cameron to make the skin shine like that on canvas.

He looked over at Cameron, who was locked onto Mone.

"What do you think?" Cameron asked.

Her gaze didn't leave the canvas. She wanted to touch it, to feel the texture. "Do I really look like this?" She bet it would be coarse, wanted to run the tips of her fingers along the edges of her face, leave some of her DNA on it for real, even a finger-print on the frame, before it was whisked away. She finally met Cameron's eyes. He smiled warmly. There were no angles in his look.

Dub watched his girl frozen in the moment. "You look better than that," Dub said. But neither of them turned to acknowledge him.

COOKOUTS

Auntie Sammy, on my mom's side, put out red-velvet cake, the real shit. Not that she had the time to make it herself, breadwinning at GlaxoSmithKline while her husband, my uncle Eddy, moved slow up the state trooper ranks from officer to corporal with dreams of lieutenant, but she had bought some, good cake too, from the Hill. My mom's side, Italian and white as ricotta, which none of us fucked with, was in love with the Hill. All Italians were. The neighborhood was a vestige of Providence's wiseguy past—bakeries that sold out of everything but spinach pies by noon, courtyard fountains that ran water on Sundays crowded with scamorza-faced nonnas. All the family on my mom's side were headed for that fate—all women, and all with scowls heavy enough to knock your eyes away. There were two blood uncles too, but one was dead, and Vinny didn't live in the state and nobody talked about him.

With Madie out of town, my long-ago ex, Kalli, had come to the party with me and was looking at the cake the same way I clocked her body—like she was thirsty and the cake was a tall-boy before close in the kitchen. She wore a loose orange shirt and tight white shorts that made her brown skin look edible everywhere in between. My aunts flashed glances at the clothes their skin tone wouldn't let them get away with, though maybe my auntie Mary could've—she showed the most Bari in her blood. Maybe my nonna when she was younger. I watched her take a slice of cheese from an antipasto plate in the making. Her skin was paler now, her back curving, giving in to gravity.

Kalli and I had been on and off since high school. Her mom had showed mine how to make stewed oxtail, even took her to the one grocery store that sold cuts of it for cheap, attached to the only Jamaican restaurant in the city, off Broad Street.

In the seven years since we'd graduated, we'd grown apart— not enough to talk about who we were fucking or loving, like we were actually grown, but enough to know not to ask. I shouldn't have been thinking any of these things anyway, because my girlfriend, Madie, was on a train back from her family's summer home in Connecticut and she didn't deserve that.

"Go get a slice," I told Kalli.

She surveyed the patio like there were cake operatives involved. But it was just my family and she knew them well.

"We haven't even had dinner," she said.

"It's a fucking cookout. Not a gala."

She cut her eyes at me but turned back to the cake. Meanwhile, my family moved around the patio setting out food in the September heat that was trying to act like it was still July.

I imagined Madie, every long blue-blooded inch of her, drinking and twirling and helping my aunts with the party, throwing slight shots at me to get on my mom's good side. I should've gone to her family estate for Labor Day weekend, but in truth, her parents were the type of white folks who try too hard, tell you how much they love Obama, get self-righteous when they talk shit about stop-and-frisk. I hadn't known Connecticut had country before I met Madie. I hadn't known a lot of things about rich folks. I liked the way she broke finance down in layman's terms. I liked waking up next to her. I told myself that she hadn't inherited all the rest.

Some of my boys' families had left Pawtucket for Hartford or New Haven, but one moved to Danielson. That place is the sticks though. Madie's parents' place in the country is all the way across the state and the feel is different. When I visited my boy in Danielson, back in high school, people sat around the same as we did. My boys and I chopped it up with some Laotians who danced better than we did and smoked more too. At a party up that way, I got it in with a girl who wore gold-trimmed Air Forces and whose friend came to get her halfway through but ended up just watching us finish.

Years later, when I first saw Madie's parents' place in Salisbury, it was like the sun set for only us, lowering itself slow behind the hills, throwing different shades into the sky to preserve our silence. The land made you say corny shit like that. That's the difference between country and sticks. Country is manicured, made pretty for someone. Sticks just happen and you drive through them quick or stop to get gas and look around at folks suffocating the same as the people you came up with. Or maybe I was wrong about it all, but grocery shopping at the corner store is a bad look regardless. Maybe you're like me and your boys used to think your spot was a palace because it had two bedrooms and only two people.

When we stayed in the country, Madie and I had our quiet moments when her parents weren't there, planning days around each other, doing our own thing and drifting back together, enjoying our own orbit. When night finally came, we'd go back inside. She'd head up the front stairs while I moved into the kitchen to crack a beer. After a few sips, I'd go up the side stairs to find her waiting. There was always more than one way to go in her homes—more doors than in a *Scooby-Doo* chase scene.

Dub had made it out to Madie's for a huge Fourth of July party a little over a year back. He knew some of the people I went to college with from a weekend in the city with me. He slipped away from the party at some point, though, and almost a full day later I found him in town with his shirt torn and bloody. I asked if he'd walked and he asked for eggs. I bought him breakfast. Dub was extra, it's true, but I didn't think my Cornell people gave him a fair shake. They were used to house-hand types.

At Madie's he'd heard me talking about some of the new music I'd been listening to. Sitting at that heartland diner, he asked me what the fuck I'd done on Vampire Weekend, not realizing it was a band name. Then he spat in his water glass and fell asleep in the booth. I'd been trying to make amends in the few years since shit had gone south between us in the city. But we'd only gotten worse.

I hadn't seen him since the previous fall when we ended up throwing hands at our boy's apartment. Laughing on my aunt's patio now, trying not to sweat, I felt the distance.

KALLI WAS A few wines deep and eating the cake with her hands and I was loving her for that. Until recently, I'd still been able to get her wet and make her laugh. Even with the series of minor and major heartbreaks I'd dealt her through the years, we still had a pulse from before. But since she'd been home, she'd been brushing me off, probably because she knew about Madie the way millennials know about the Cold War.

"Lili-bear?"

She threw some shade my way.

"My likkle beef patty," I said, to no response.

We were in our mid-twenties, on that self-defining bullshit, but her face still looked high-school-young. She slumped into the patio furniture and her thighs billowed along the edges of her white shorts. She caught me looking and shook her finger like Dikembe Mutombo. Even though she was there to catch up with my family, wearing those shorts was no accident.

Still, she was right. I shouldn't have been looking. My mind wandered back to Madie sitting with her family on their veranda by the pool. The place I should've been. But her parents always asked me about the mayor of New York and I could never tell if they meant to ask me about his high-yaller family or his policy, so usually I came out sounding like an idiot. The only way that would change was if I was around them more.

Kalli crossed her legs. The family-time fantasy drowned with the swiftness. I got up and moved a folding chair closer to her, draped an awkward arm across her shoulders. They felt small under me.

"You thought," she said and moved my arm off.

Even leaning away from me, she smelled good, a little too sweet, but if I licked her neck I'd taste the salt. When we had first started dating, her mom would bring over gizzada and sit with my mom and nonna downstairs, listening closely while Kalli and I "studied" in my room. My bed was too loud to have sex on, so we'd move to the floor, though there wasn't much of it in that old house, and go slow so I had to look in her eyes and smell the perfume and sweat on her neck, which is probably how I caught feelings in the first place.

"What's wrong?" I said.

She moved her plate. She'd peeled the frosting off, and it was in chunks everywhere. Then her eyes found the sky, the house, the trees, the other guests, the sun, really anything but my face.

"You got a new man?" I tried to smile.

She didn't, I hoped. I hadn't seen her in months. We'd talked on the phone now and again, but she hadn't been home much since I'd moved back. I'd explained to Madie that we were just friends, and that was true. She'd told me about the protests and rallies she'd been a part of. I didn't know if it was to brag or just to shoot the shit and avoid the personal.

"No new niggas," I sang.

She mean-mugged me. She wasn't about that word. Back in the day, she'd told me that her family never threw *nigga* around. I told her, If you're black in America for long enough, it's hard not to start. I had some friends from college that used the word like a blanket, for punctuation in mixed company, for armor. My mom's side had never heard me talk that way, never heard the way my boys and I passed it around like a dutch, all of us wrapped in it.

"Do you really want to know?" Kalli said.

I looked out at the trees lining the property. Two acres of English-garden-style high grass rolled out from Sammy's porch. A few young trees were staked to keep them safe from storms. The oaks in Madie's parents' yard had been there for centuries. I wondered if folks hunted near my aunt's here in Warwick. It was still early for geese, but they'd be gearing up in Ithaca. Some days I thought about moving back, but Madie had made it clear that it'd be the end of our thing. Plus, I was in a good kitchen in Cranston, learning under the Montalbanos, Rhode Island restaurant royalty.

Eddy flipped some meat on the grill in front of us. My auntie Liza put a glass cover over the cake and Kalli set her plate of crumbs down. My mom mixed a drink she didn't need—she was small and new to booze in general. But having always been the black sheep among her own kin, she was greasing the wheels. I could understand that.

"'Cause I'll tell you if you really want to know," Kalli said.

Eddy started yelling like he was battling the six-burner Weber. The sausage smelled good but it was just the fat dripping. His dumb ass was trying to cook the links on high like they were fucking steaks. He hadn't even slit them and I waited for them to pop and burn. He was talking about his job and how no one knew how tough it was. He transitioned into the loaded weapons he kept around the house. "Everyone wants to be a cop killer," he said. "Go to the Dominican parade and watch how they look at me."

My uncles kept talking open and loud. They were heavy in the sauce by then and didn't notice Kalli and me listening.

Uncle Bill, Liza's husband, nodded. He was rich-person fat, before you get so much money that you get skinny again, and wore an open silk shirt. "They turn every dead man into a saint," he said.

Kalli looked across her face at me.

I shrugged. "Family."

Sammy offered some antipasto, but Eddy waved her away. She looked at him like he was her tenant.

Kalli was silent and I could see my image wilting in her eyes, which was twisted because I'd never judged her for her crazy-ass relatives. Families come with bullshit, everybody knows that. I imagined my younger sister, Whitney, throwing some shots at

Eddy. But at sixteen, she wasn't truly indignant. She used race more as a weapon to make white folks back down. Plus it was a Labor Day cookout and I didn't feel like going on a Black Power crusade. I wondered if Jamaican holidays were as bloody as American ones. I was cotton-mouthed, wanted a beer. But my mom was standing by the cooler and I didn't want to hear about it later. Plus, she was giving Kalli and me space. I didn't know if it was courtesy or because she'd never gotten over Kalli and hoped the time alone would rekindle us. Kalli's eyes were cutting. She'd always made me stand up straight and I didn't want to lose that.

"I'm going to get some wine," she said. "Want anything?"

"Yeah, get my dashiki off the rack."

She gave me the finger, then fixed her shorts and left.

SOMETIMES I WISHED Dub had never introduced us. All week, since she'd been in town, Kalli and I had chopped it up about our high-school days, but at a distance, like we were no longer in on the same jokes. I'd been stuck on how things had gone down between Dub and me. All she said was, People change. I even got a shape-up at Atomic, the shop we used to go to for cuts. It'd been a long time and none of the barbers knew my name anymore.

Kalli came back with white wine filled too high in her glass. She swung her hips forward more than walked—sexy, but unsteady-looking. I fixed my eyes on my phone to avoid staring.

Madie's last message read *Be home soon, dear*. I hated when she used that fifties slang with me. It was her way of writing off whatever I had to say. I thought about our life together—almost a year now. We'd been together for two, but sharing a bathroom is when it gets serious. The worst of getting to know each other was over. She had some lactose intolerance, but nothing a thick blanket couldn't solve. She loved the Kings of Leon and would definitely fuck the lead singer if given the chance, but nothing could solve that, everyone's got some crush. I imagined Josephine Baker in that banana skirt often. One of my boys once told me, *Never think you got someone's heart on lock, there is always a nigga with a spare key.* Later I found out Pac said it first. As far as Madie's faults, I couldn't think of much else. She broke the world into lists of pros and cons and neat angles. But everything tended to blend together for me, so we worked well enough. Kalli liked to make lists too, but she also yelled in public and was forward with strangers, some shit Madie would never do. I missed that. I wondered how I measured up to Madie's exes. If I was the type to go through her shit, I'm sure I could've found a neatly written list.

Kalli sat down in a different lawn chair across from me and took a deep swallow, swished the wine like a marathon runner, only she didn't spit it back out.

"That glass family-style?" I said.

"Do you get your jokes off cereal boxes?" she said.

"Nah, I get them from your blog."

She stoned up at that. She wrote, time to time, for a "New Black" website and had her own social justice Tumblr.

"Kuul yu fut, Queen Nzinga. I'm fucking with you." I pulled the glass from her hand and sipped heavy. It tasted awful. White wine always did. I gave it back.

Kalli ignored me and checked her phone. She was too far away for me to see the screen. The wineglass looked oversize in her other hand. The light from her phone was bright enough to show a zit smothered in makeup on the right side of her chin. Auntie Lucy had lit tiki torches to keep the mosquitoes away. They didn't work for shit but looked good in the fading light.

"Important text?" I said.

Kalli sipped her wine again and said nothing. She didn't know how serious Madie and I had gotten, and I was sure she wasn't without.

"He ain't better-looking than me," I said.

She put down her wine and held her pointer fingers about a foot apart.

"Lyin' ass," I said.

"Fine, don't believe me."

"Don't say that shit. It's a holiday." I grabbed my dick. "Plus you love Richard, don't lie."

"First off, Labor Day isn't a real holiday," she said. "And keep telling yourself that."

"Links are up," Eddy said.

My family liquored up. Eddy's mom and sister, Sheila and Dela, drank Sambuca and spoke Greek to each other. We waited by the grill for the meat, then Kalli and I sat down across from each other at the enormous dining table on the patio. The table was big enough to seat fourteen, like Sammy was trying to one-up the Last Supper. An arrangement of fresh flowers sat in the center like a picture straight out of a home magazine. My mom grew peonies, and I was proud of her for making us a home. I leaned forward and touched the soft, off-white petals but didn't know what they were. I wasn't the type to know what bloomed in September. Even if I were, I would've lied. The table probably cost more than all her furniture combined.

"Who moves this in the winter?" I looked at the table legs, Serena Williams thick.

Eddy said they would just refinish it in the fall and tarp it down. He was a loud son of a bitch.

"Hurricanes?" I said.

"A hurricane isn't budging this."

Kalli chewed loud on some cocktail shrimp and I hoped she'd get drunk enough to forget we weren't in high school anymore. I wished I could live what we had again, but I knew there was no salvation in it, no simplicity.

Kalli sucked the tails out of their shells like no one was watching, used her fingers and teeth to pry them open. She was sitting next to my mom, who was asking about her law-school applications, wide-eyed, like Kalli's words were the elixir of youth. I imagined Kalli in a sundress, her hair straightened, a woman to worship. The fabric would hide her body, make her look smaller. Madie was tall. She had pictures from her older sister's wedding, where she'd been a bridesmaid. The dress was turquoise and didn't read well on her pale skin, but she was beautiful anyway—it seemed the photographer had pumped the sun with extra light, and her eyes with extra blue. She looked ready to step into a horse-drawn carriage, her long brown hair pulled back and shining. When black folks say we're kings and queens, I wonder how many of us imagine white faces.

I checked my phone to see if Madie had texted again.

"Put that away!" my nonna said. She smiled, then started in on the sausage, ripping through the casing like string cheese.

"Hey, hey, we didn't say grace!"

Everyone turned to my aunt Liza, the youngest of my mom's four sisters.

"Go ahead, Brown Bear," she said.

Kalli cocked her head at me.

"Damn, Auntie, it's a cookout, not Easter."

"Just say the goddamned grace," Eddy said.

"Eddy!"

"Eddy!"

There was a minor chorus.

"Yeah, Brown Bear, just say grace." Kalli smirked.

"You g'wan say it," I said. She ignored the comment. I put my fork down.

Say it, bitch, Kalli mouthed.

I smiled. Bill and Lucy held out their hands, which felt warm and dry in mine. My mom's family varied in their Catholicness. Mom wasn't the grace-saying type herself, but I wanted to eat so I got on with it.

"Let us bow our heads," I started. "Lord God, we'd like to thank You for this bounty. This beautiful blessing You've laid before us. To thank You also for the hands that prepared it."

I opened my eyes. Everyone else's were closed tight, even Kalli's.

"Thank You for the love we share," I said, "and the family we share it with. And thank You for the fortune you've bestowed upon us."

I *was* thankful that my family could throw down in the kitchen and afford food this nice. That I was still alive when men in my pops' family were prone to die young. That my sister's head was above water. I was thankful for a lot, really. My lungs were clear. People's heads were still bowed. Bill's hand felt weird in mine. We'd never touched before. My mom's side wasn't the touching type.

"Thank You, Lord, for Your protection." I was far from being worthy of God's protection, but I still prayed for it. "And please protect those who need it more than us. So many need it more than us on this day, Lord. Those without the blessing of food. Those without the greater blessing of kin."

My family stirred. Bill tried to squeeze the hippie out of my hand. All of a sudden I could hear the clock-hand tick of a sprinkler in the neighbors' yard. I zoned deep into prayer, like something tipping and pouring.

"Lord, bring us justice. Bring it to all of us."

Eyes were still closed. Bill's hand tightened even more, but it didn't shake me. I thought of Kalli sitting across from me and kept going.

"Guide those who need guidance to do right by You. 'Cause Your law is not our law. Our laws serve a few and Your laws serve many. Please bring us into the light so that we may understand Your divine will. Bring us into the light so that we may live up to Your image. Let us not just speak justice's name, let us live it. And punish those who've not upheld their duty to protect."

"Okay—" Lucy said.

I stopped and my family opened their eyes and started to eat slow. No one looked at me. Kalli said, "Amen," and I wanted to laugh—her sense of humor hadn't changed. Bill was attacking a chicken breast before I could even make sense of the shift.

"Dela, get me more Sambuca," Sheila said.

"Ma, I just got you some," Dela said.

"It's gone."

Eddy glared at me as I started in on the dry-ass sausage. Nonna was already deep in hers. Kalli drank and turned to my auntie Mary, whose basement my boys and I used to chief in back in high school. She had either turned a blind eye or was blind for real, and either way I appreciated her for it. Conversations started up again. Sheila sucked on an ice cube and Eddy downed his drink.

Lucy turned to me and nodded across the table. "You should marry that one," she said. Lucy'd stayed with my mom, nonna, and me for a while when we first moved back east. She was upfront about that kind of shit.

Then, while we were all loud with the sounds of eating, Eddy said, "Gio, why are you so angry?"

The table fell silent.

"It was grace, Eddy," I said.

"Do you have a problem with how I make my living?"

"It was just grace," Liza said. She squirmed a little and pushed some food around her plate. As the youngest, Liza was the peacekeeper.

"If you're gonna say it," Eddy told me, "then fucking own it."

"Eddy!" Sheila said.

"Hold on, Mom," he said. And then he turned to me again. "Why do you blame everyone else for your problems?" he said.

Kalli wasn't smiling anymore. No one spoke. My cotton mouth was back.

"You attack the police?" Eddy said. "You need a cause so you make one up?"

"Attack the police? *Ha*," Kalli said, belting the *ha* that I'd always loved. It was the same one she belted when you were around your boys and talking big about how you hit it like a porn star and she overheard your bullshit lie and said you always got too high and wanted to cuddle.

I thought about how Madie would've been sitting across from me, silent, watching, taking tight sips of wine, or maybe just focusing her eyes on me with a look begging that I be quiet.

"You've been an officer?" Eddy said and glanced at Kalli.

"Jesus, Mary, and Joseph," Sheila said.

"Gio's right," my mom said, but soft, and I was mad that she didn't offer more.

Kalli's voice got louder. "Watch the news," she said.

"Do you feel persecuted?" My uncle put his fork down real deliberate and stared at Kalli.

"Don't patronize her," I said.

"There's a video of a black man strangled to death on camera," Kalli said.

"He had a heart condition," Eddy said. "And you know the officer in charge was a black woman, right?" He picked up his pork rib bone and took a massive bite.

Of course Kalli'd known, but she hunched a little in her seat.

"You don't think she felt pressured?" I said.

"She wasn't under fire," Eddy said.

"Pressured to fall in line," I said.

"She was in command."

"So?" Kalli said. "She could've been influenced."

"What, you think the academy teaches us to be racist?"

"No, America does," I said.

Eddy bit off some cartilage, spat it out. "You know how fucking dumb you sound?"

"He was choked to death," Kalli said, straightening up again.

Eddy put the bone down and picked a piece of meat out of his teeth. "Gio, remember when you got pulled over for drunk driving and Ricci had to call my cell to ask if you were my nephew? I told him you were, right?"

The sound of utensils scraping plates was loud. All other conversation and motion ceased. Here was a story that'd never been told. My mom stared at me, her worst fears confirmed. Kalli looked away.

"Right?" Eddy said again. "You don't even need to answer, of course I told him you were my nephew. I told you my badge number the day you got your license. He stopped you on the Newport Bridge, let you drive into Jamestown and park. He gave you a ride home, thirty minutes in the cruiser. You know what he'd have done if you weren't my nephew, drunk as you were?"

The sprinkler shut off in the distance.

"I knew your badge number," I said. "He didn't have to call you."

"You were drunk enough to drive off the damn bridge."

"No, I was a nigger in a Nissan," I said.

Eddy didn't miss a beat. "The police have done nothing but give you breaks," he said. "You are about as much a nigger as Derek Jeter."

My family looked at me but I went mute. Content to pretend it hadn't happened, they returned to eating. My mom avoided my gaze. She had told me the same thing many times with different language. If Kalli was light enough, she would've blushed for me.

I wanted to say something, but it was over. To them it was deaded. Eddy was already onto his second pork chop and talking to Bill.

I got up. "You want a ride home?" I asked Kalli.

"Sit down," Bill said.

"Sure," Kalli said and stood up, thanked my family for the food.

My aunts tried to say some things to get us to stay. When I got near the patio door, my nonna called out, "Brown Bear, please take some more to eat."

* * *

MADIE AND I lived in Seekonk, where the three-family homes stop and the lawns brighten up. It wasn't far from Kalli's. The houses where Sammy lived in Warwick were all *Sopranos*-type McMansions. In the dark summer night, there was only the sound of the tires on the road—too much quiet. It felt good to slide back into the city, I took a left on York and saw the cars spilling down Kalli's folks' driveway in the distance. I asked about her situation again.

"Why do you want to know about my love life?"

"'Cause I do," I said. I pulled up alongside her mailbox going the wrong way, put the car in park.

"Are you sure?"

"Fuck, either tell me or get out."

"He lives in Philly."

"Okay."

"He's a Kappa. Went to Harvard."

I unlocked the door.

"You heard enough?" she said, fucking with me.

"You'll have to introduce us," I said.

She threw me a look, pulled the handle. The lights in front of her house came on. "My dad told me to invite you in," she said.

"Tell your pops I said mi know."

She rolled her eyes.

"What's Kappa's name?"

She had one foot out the door and her orange shirt rode up again. "It doesn't matter."

"What's his name?"

"Bishop."

"The nigga from *Juice*?"

She turned to avoid laughing.

"How long are you in town?" I asked.

"A few more days." She closed the door and took a couple of steps toward her house. The porch light turned her to a silhouette. Another ghost was born between us. The same one that stood next to her at the anti–police brutality rallies I never attended. A ghost that would've avoided a cookout of loud-mouthed wops, or maybe stayed to scrap.

WHEN I CAME in, Madie was on the couch in her panties and one of my T-shirts. It felt too hot for any clothes at all, but she was calm and comfortable, listening to reggae while she read. She was going through an Americans-in-Paris phase—Stein, Dos Passos, Cole Porter. Senior year of high school, I used to cut class and sit in the empty gym reading *Manhattan Transfer*.

After a beat, Madie looked up from her book. "What's wrong?" she said.

My bloodshot eyes shone heavy in the mirror that hung on the opposite wall. She patted the seat next to her. She always told me the smell of my clothes made her wet. I imagined her touching herself with my clothes on. I sat and leaned my head back.

She massaged my temples. "Dinner was rough?" She moved her hands down to the base of my skull. "Take some cleansing breaths."

I remembered the day cops had rolled up on Dub and me in my own driveway. We were fourteen and had just finished a game of one-on-one on the hoop outside. My mom would park on the street every day so I could get some shots up. Dub and I were sitting on the asphalt throwing pebbles at each other and talking shit about the game.

He saw the lights instant and told me to get up and walk inside slow. He knew what was going on before I could even clock it.

I hadn't made it ten yards when the cop asked me where I was going.

"Home," I said.

He laughed.

I wished I'd told Eddy that story, but I thought that if Dub hadn't been there, maybe it wouldn't have been anything.

Madie stopped massaging my head. The apartment windows were open. The summer insects hummed heavy.

"You don't have to stop that," I said.

"It's all or none. You have to communicate, baby. I'm a package deal."

I got up and she asked where I was going.

"To get a glass of wine," I said.

"Don't angry-drink," she said.

"I feel like a drink."

"Talk to me." She looked straight into me.

"You want one?"

"Yes." She smiled like I'd caught her stealing cookies. Her whole face brightened.

I leaned down and kissed her. She knew how to make me hard with just her lips, barely touching me, staying almost out of reach. She would let her lips hover near mine, wait for me to lose control.

I came back with two large mugs of wine and the bottle, downed mine, then poured another.

"Relax on the shine, General," she said.

She had a thousand phrases like that. She said her family in

South Carolina used them but they sounded like make-believe. She went hard on her own mug and asked again what had happened. She rubbed the base of my neck and asked if it was about her. I stayed silent, starting to feel good and relaxed from the wine.

"Gio?"

"What?"

"What happened?"

"Tomorrow," I said. "I'm too tired." I held up the bottle of wine. There was about a third left.

"How is Labor Day contentious?" she said. "The Fourth, sure. Christmas, of course. But what did you argue about? Unions?"

I just wanted to sit with her, but I kept replaying the night. "It got heavy," I said.

She rolled her eyes and started to lick my ear. I loved when she did that and she knew it. She gave me the backs of her hands to kiss, then her palms, then the tips of her fingers. Blood rushed back into me. She swung one leg over and felt me. Her bare thighs were so pale. She kissed me for a while in her teasing way before she unbuckled me. My focus shifted quick. I rolled her onto her back, kissed all the way down to her feet, and stayed there kissing the tops of her toes and massaging her legs. Licked the arch of her foot. I made my way back up slowly. She raised her hips so I could slip her panties off. I caught her scent again and turned so hard it almost hurt. I kissed her between her legs, but I couldn't wait. I finished undressing myself. My body—broad and brown—reflected in the mirror that hung across from me. I pulled her up and made her look at us in the mirror, my body even darker beside her milky frame. I didn't feel like a king, I felt like a pillager. I bent her forward on the couch.

"Beg me," I said.

She gasped and closed her eyes.

I reached my hand down and teased her—just a fingertip. I stopped. Her blue eyes were wide and I flipped her in one motion.

"Beg me," I said.

"Fuck me," she said.

I slid a hand down to her throat and the words came out: "Tell me to fuck you like a nigger."

Her face twisted. "What?" She tried to sit up to get away from me, but I was on her, my right hand moving from her throat to her collarbone.

"Say it." I reached my other hand down to tease her, touch her with my fingers. She sagged under the pressure of my body and winced. "Tell me."

"Please stop," she said. Her voice trailed off, so weak it got lost in the reggae still playing.

"You like it," I said. "Tell me you like it." I held her down and kept repeating myself until her skin started to turn red under my weight and I thought she was going to cry. I went to go inside her. "Tell me I'm your nigger."

She was squirming wildly to get away, but my size made it difficult. She tried using her feet to push me off but couldn't. Our bodies were too close.

"Say it!" I had my hand on her throat again, stronger now. She reached up to push my face but my arms were too long. She clawed at my shoulders. I let go of her throat and pinned her arms down at the biceps and she whimpered, then bit my forearm deep enough to break the skin. I let go for a second. She slapped my face and I fell back on the couch from shock. Her legs draped over me. We were both short of breath. She stared at me.

I looked down at myself, still hard from the thought of it. I lifted her left ankle and felt the softness of her skin there. I kissed the bottom of her arch. She pulled her foot away and curled into a ball, her therapist-calm spent.

Some strands of her brown hair were visible in the mirror barely above my jawline. I went to kiss the top of her head but she kept me at arm's length. I was too spent to push further and rested my head on her raised hip. She got up and left to the bedroom. After a few seconds, there was the sound of something being dragged out of the closet and thrown onto the bed. The pull of the heavy zipper came first, then the scrape of hangers being pushed along the bar in the closet, methodic and slow. She crossed the small hallway between our bedroom and the bathroom. The vent fan turned on almost loud enough to drown the noise of her emptying the cabinet of her things. My stomach was tight with nerves. I pulled the shirt she'd left over my eyes. But there was no sleep, only my breath inside the shirt on a hot night. Madie dug in the bowl where we kept change and phone chargers and keys. The screen door slammed closed behind her because I'd never fixed the spring.

The night filled to the top with making and changing plans and grand gestures to get her back that would never work because she wasn't that type of woman, with me editing every memory of us and every story that came before, back to my childhood, down to the immutable. She got sick of being haunted by ghosts she'd never even met.

Acknowledgments

I promised some homies if this day ever came, I'd be on a Kanye "Last Call" type tangent with the acknowledgments. I don't want to break that promise. So first and foremost, let me reiterate that this is through the grace of the dearly beloved ghosts—I hope they would've been proud of this work. I miss you immensely.

I won't do these acknowledgments numbered 'cause it'd be inaccurate. With that being said, I owe my life to my mother and grandmother for both their undying love and foresight. My mom told me the ball would stop bouncing. It still bounces, but I don't jump very good anymore (the homies will say I never did, but they're full of shit), so she was right on that one. I'm glad she kept putting books in my hands when so many folks around me were on a different path. To my grandma, thanks for the help with everything when times were tough and for being a fountain of wisdom throughout the years. Phillip is thankful even if you think he stays complaining.

I am endlessly appreciative for my cousins, outstanding men

in a world that needs them. They are more like brothers, truly, guiding stars, blessed with my aunts' warmth and strength. In this country we are inundated with images of black men as criminals, but my cousins held it down with love, straight talk, and honesty. And for that, they are invaluable role models to me.

Thanks to my other brothers: Zig, Ryan, and Ryan, and Es dot. For the couches to crash on and the support throughout the years. This book wouldn't be possible without the things we got into and light you all possess. So happy to see you all doing your thing too. Es, good looks on the artwork for this book too. Even if we don't meet the deadlines. I'm joyous that we could link and make that happen. The work was beautiful.

Shout out to Walz too, whose motivation motivates me, and for the slew of pirated music. That shit was the sound track to some of these stories, homie. I've got no doubt that you're up next.

To cousin Kenan, thanks for the perspective on some things that had me twisted, and a dope basement to crash at when Milwaukee was testing my patience. Also for being a shining example of family success for a kid who didn't have many of them. Congratulations on fatherhood × 2.

Big Fonz! Speaking of the illest families, supreme gratitude to you and yours for all the guidance and overly solicited legal advice...ha. Your family is full of grace and wisdom and they ain't stingy with it. Love you, bro.

To the Garys, and especially Trina, I feel so blessed that you became a part of my life when you did. And Trina, thank you for my first teaching gig (I imagine you threw your full weight into the ring to get me hired on that one). Your family is one of the rarest I've encountered—so clear-eyed and kind. You really planted a seed that inspired me to dream about a better education system and it changed my life so positively. My experiences at PoCC and SDLC will surely find their way into writing someday in some shape or form. But I'll probably leave out the part where I cry on the bus home.

In that vein, I need to thank a lot of the folks at Pingree and Prep@Pingree for modeling what caring and driven educators look like. I'm so appreciative too for my former students who have become part of my inner circle. Watching y'all grow up and succeed has been amazing. The talent and goodness y'all possess is remarkable. Thanks for keeping me young(ish). Ed Kloman, thanks for being the craziest, awesome old white dude I've ever met and one of the most voracious readers and inspiring teachers. In a different life, you would've been a battle rapper with those oratory skills. To Michelle, Daughter of January, for showing me what hard work in the classroom looks like and for sharing so much of your knowledge to make sure I didn't fail as a teacher my first year... and of course for continually cutting me down to size. To the Estys, thank you so much for inviting me into your home while I was teaching and still trying to find my way toward this project. Also for showing me that nature can be dope.

To my sisters, Lauri and Juuuj, thanks for being proud of me even when I struggled to be proud of myself, for being excited when I was washed out, and for being confident when I was nervous. I owe a lot of my peace of mind to your efforts. Also, shout out to Juuuj on the author photo for making ya boy look pretty. Glad we could make good on that promise we made as seventeen-year-olds, even doper that the powers that be let us make it happen on a summer day on the banks of the Spree.

Next, and also first, *huge* thanks to my literary mother, Amity Gaige, for telling me I could do this thing here for real. I remember when I got into Iowa and I called you immediately. You sighed in relief and said, "Good, I'm not crazy." Well, thanks for being willing to be crazy before anyone else saw merit in my work. And for keeping me sane throughout the process when this passion turned into business. If not for you, I'd be somewhere else doing something different.

To my other literary guardian angels, Rebecca Makkai, Ayana Mathis, and Ethan Canin, thank you for the lessons and blessings and for paying off the gatekeepers of this here industry with your stamps of approval.

Biggest thanks to my big lil sis Cat P, for making me continue to believe in the goodness of others and myself and for keeping me equal parts sane and insane. Thank you for convincing me to keep writing and for letting me tell you stories about my family that I've never told. Couldn't have made this book without your voice and love.

I also need to thank the good folks at the workshop for all the knowledge and dedication they possess and the seriousness with which they study the craft and the support I was given, both financial and technical. Special shout to Sean Adams for his keen eye and notes. To my big-hearted brethren Tim, I'm so thankful for your positivity in my life. So happy that you've found happiness and love. And so unnecessarily full from the heavensent dishes that you throw down in the kitchen. Griddle Boys for life. To Deb, Jan, and Connie for holding the front office down and providing a dose of reality in a land where we all got our heads in the clouds.

Then of course, the actual gatekeepers, starting with Anna

"the Dreamweaver" Stein for taking a chance on my work and going to bat for me. All the people at Little, Brown who saw the vision and wanted to make it a reality. With a special thanks to Ben George for his diligence even though some days were a battle. I know you went to war for this book and for that I am infinitely grateful. Also to Lena Little for coaching me through a publicity process that has me sweating through my shirts. I am eternally grateful for your faith and efforts.

And last and most first, to Willa H**b**y, I will forever be in your debt for the unfaltering love and support and a critical voice even when I don't want to hear it but need to hear it most. You made the work better. You made me better too, and still do. What's a book worth when compared with a life? I love you and owe you both.

Last, last, to hip-hop, the sound track to my life and the way I found my voice in the first place. Hopefully, the early days freestyling and sharpening the delivery have paid off and the bounce has made its way into some of these pages.

To the readers who made it this far, thanks for indulging me.

With love,
Jeff

About the Author

JM Holmes was born in Denver and raised in Rhode Island. He is a Pushcart Prize winner and a graduate of the Iowa Writers' Workshop. His stories have appeared in the *Paris Review*, the *White Review*, the *Missouri Review*, the *Gettysburg Review*, and *H.O.W.* This is his first book. He lives in Milwaukee and is currently at work on a novel.